Books by David Baddiel

ANIMALCOLM

BIRTHDAY BOY

HEAD KID

THE PARENT AGENCY

THE PERSON CONTROLLER

DAVID
BADDIEL

Illustrated by Steven Lenton

HarperCollins *Children's Books*

First published in Great Britain by
HarperCollins Children's Books in 2018
HarperCollins Children's Books is a division of HarperCollinsPublishers Ltd,
HarperCollins Publishers
1 London Bridge Street
London SE1 9GF

The HarperCollins website address is
www.harpercollins.co.uk

1

Text copyright © David Baddiel 2018
Illustrations copyright © Steven Lenton 2018
All rights reserved.

HARDBACK ISBN 978–0–00–820052–7

TRADE PAPERBACK ISBN 978–0–00–820053–4

David Baddiel and Steven Lenton assert the moral right to be

identified as the author and illustrator of the work respectively.

Typeset in ITC Novarese point 12/22
Printed and bound in England by CPI Group (UK) Ltd, Croydon, CR0 4YY

MIX
Paper from
responsible sources

FSC
www.fsc.org

FSC™ C007454

This book is produced from independently certified FSC™ paper
to ensure responsible forest management.

For more information visit: www.harpercollins.co.uk/green

To Enzo, for the idea

OFFHEAD

Office for Fine High Education

and Daftness-proofing

BRACKET WOOD SCHOOL REPORT

Summary of findings:

[INADEQUATE]

Detailed findings:

TEACHING: Poor (especially Mr Barrington).

FACILITIES: Not good.

FOOD: Inedible.

STAFF MORALE: Low.

EXAM SUCCESS: Please don't ask.

TOILETS: Appalling.

RANKING AND RECOMMENDATIONS: See overleaf.

CHAPTER 1

Inadequate

Bracket Wood School had never, since it was opened all the way back in 1983, received an OFFHEAD ranking of Outstanding. Nor had it received one of Good. There was a very brief golden period, in the early 90s, when it received one of Satisfactory. But then that was found to have been a mistake – the inspector had ticked the wrong box, for which he himself got marked down to Not As Good As We Thought – and it went back to its usual ranking: Inadequate.

It was, in fact, a running joke in the OFFHEAD offices – not a place where you'd have thought there'd be much joking, but at least on the subject of Bracket Wood you'd be wrong – that one day they might have to create a new ranking for this particular school: Rubbish.

This was a problem for Bracket Wood because OFFHEAD, as I'm sure you all know, is a government organisation which checks that schools *aren't* rubbish. Parents, as you also might know, pay a lot of attention to their reports. Some parents, in fact, spend far too much of their time reading OFFHEAD reports, and discussing them with their friends who are also parents, and worrying all the time about which school to send their children to, based on OFFHEAD reports. Some parents worry about this so much they ruin their child's childhood. But that's another story.

This story begins with the staff and governors and parents and even some of the pupils at Bracket Wood in something of a panic. Because OFFHEAD was coming. In a month's time. Which was even more worrying than usual. For two reasons:

1. Bracket Wood Council, Education Department, had announced, on hearing that OFFHEAD was coming again, that if the school got another Inadequate rating it might be time to think about closing the place down, and . . .

2. Ryan Ward.

CHAPTER 2
A Prince Among Pranksters

"**R**ight, Six B!" said Mr Barrington, moving the TV monitor into place on top of his desk. "It's good news. Today we are going to watch a TV For Schools documentary."

A groan went up from the class.

"Stop groaning!" said Mr Barrington.

Another groan went up from the class.

"I said, stop groaning. I didn't say groan again."

"Is it *A World Without Lead*?" said Barry Bennett.

"No. Although that *was* very good," said Mr Barrington, putting the DVD into the player. "Especially the bit showing what a problem that would be for cable sheathing."

"Not that one about dust! Please!" said Sam Green.

"*It Gets Everywhere!* you mean? I'll have you know that won a DAFTA!"

"Do you mean a BAFTA?"

"No, it's an award from the Dust And Filth Trackers Association."

"Please not *A Shepherd's World* . . ."

"Just be quiet and turn the lights off, Malcolm Bailey – and don't tell me you didn't love the twenty minutes in that documentary about how various types of grass taste to a sheep."

Malcolm shook his head quite certainly – as if he really knew about *that* – and turned off the light. A menu appeared on the screen. It showed a large metal bucket. And the words: *"How Buckets Are Made"*.

"What's this one about, sir?" said Morris Fawcett, the head teacher's son, who frankly had little hope of following in his father's footsteps academically.

"Well, Morris, I'm glad you asked me that. It's about how— Hold on, are you being sarcastic?"

"I wish he was," said his twin sister Isla wearily.

"Hmm," said Mr Barrington, pressing *Play*. "Just watch. It's very interesting."

With that, he went and sat – as he always did after putting boring documentaries on for 6B to watch – on his chair behind the TV, pushed his enormous glasses up on his forehead and fell asleep.

At which point, Ryan Ward, who had been sitting at the back quietly, knew it was time to make his move.

"What are you writing?" whispered Ellie Stone. She was one of six pupils gathered in a circle round

Mr Barrington's right hand. The reason this circle had gathered was that Mr Barrington's right hand was lying loosely by his side. His head was lolling on his chest and he was snoring gently into his moustache. A tiny bit of dribble, originating from the left-hand corner of 6B's teacher's mouth, had made its way down to the top of his chin. And crouching by his right hand was Ryan Ward, brandishing an eyeliner pencil.

"You'll see . . ." said Ryan, whispering back.

"And so the sheet metal is curved round the frame of the bucket . . ." said the television, not whispering.

Very carefully, and making sure he did it gently enough not to wake his teacher, he began to write.

"That's clever," said Sam. "You're doing mirror writing."

"I am," said Ryan. He carried on writing with great concentration. Because this was, of course, a prank. And Ryan, the naughtiest boy at Bracket Wood, prided himself on his pranks. He was a philosopher-prince amongst pranksters. Not for him the bucket of water on the top of the door, or the fifty pizzas delivered to your house that you haven't ordered. He was a prankster whose motto was *Make it new.* Even if he was using an old trick – such as one you might play on a sleeping teacher – Ryan would have to do it in his own way. The devil, some people say, is in the detail, and certainly this particular devil always made sure he got *all* the details right for *all* his tricks.

"It's important, at this stage, to make sure that the bottom of the bucket does not have a hole in it. Even if later – ha-ha! – you might want to sing a song about that!"

Ryan put the eyeliner pencil down.

"OK," he said – still whispering – to his little audience. "Now for the kicker."

He reached into his school bag and brought out a little plastic box. Inside, munching on a piece of lettuce, was an ant. He put his index finger inside the box and let the ant crawl on to it. Then, watched by the entranced circle of schoolmates, he carefully raised that finger towards Mr Barrington's forehead, to just above his pushed-up glasses. The ant looked up, twitched its tiny antennae and began to make its way down his finger.

"Using this process, a workshop can make up to fifteen buckets a day."

"Hang on," said a voice. "Are you doing what I think you're doing . . . ?"

CHAPTER 3

No Worries

Ryan didn't turn round. Focused, concentrating, he kept his finger still.

"I don't know, Dionna," said Ryan. "What do you think I'm doing?"

Dionna Baxter, standing right behind him, was Ryan's best friend. She was also usually his prank assistant. But that didn't mean she saw herself as junior to him. Not least because she was two months older.

"I think you're doing something that means that ant is gonna die."

"Well . . . possibly . . ." said Ryan.

"Can't do that," said Dionna.

"What?"

"Can't do that, Ryan. Not fair to the ant. Little ant just strolling around your garden, building its ant stuff, carrying leaves . . ."

"Actually, it was carrying one of my bogies. That's how I caught it. Couldn't resist that salty goodness."

"Whatevs. Point is, it doesn't deserve what you've got planned. Mr B, maybe. Not the ant."

"Dionna," said Ryan, still looking at the ant, which by now had nearly made it to the teacher's forehead, "if we keep arguing, Barrington will wake up!"

"So. Stop arguing."

Finally, Ryan moved his gaze up to meet Dionna's. Her eyes looked at him in a way that brooked no argument.

Ryan sighed. "OK. OK!" He put his finger back down into the plastic box with the lettuce in it. The ant, uncertain as to the point of its journey to and from the box, crawled off and resumed munching.

"So *now* what are we going to use to tickle him?" said Ryan.

"No worries," said Dionna. She went round behind Mr Barrington's still-sleeping form and flicked her head down, making the front tips of her hair fall on to his forehead. She moved her head from side to side, drawing the strands gently across his ingrained frown lines.

Mr Barrington twitched in his sleep. His nose wiggled. Ryan, watching, understood.

"OK, everyone! Back to your seats! Now!"

Everyone ran, and they all got there in time. In time, that is, to see – in one movement – Mr Barrington open his eyes, let his glasses fall back down on to his nose and slap the palm of his right hand hard across his forehead.

He yawned, stood up and said, "Hmm. Right, class!"

He was about to say, "That was a very interesting documentary. I hope you all enjoyed it."

But he never got the chance as they were all pointing at him and laughing.

CHAPTER 4

Empty Space

"Sorry, Mr Barrington," said Mr Fawcett, "I didn't quite follow?"

"As I was saying, Headmaster, I was showing Six B a fascinating documentary – I was paying great attention to it myself, of course – when suddenly the whole class started laughing and pointing at me. Well, obviously, I knew straight away who was behind this mockery: Ryan Ward! As usual!"

Mr Barrington was standing in the office of

Mr Fawcett, the headmaster of Bracket Wood, in front of his desk. Next to him stood Ryan Ward. There is an expression: *as if butter wouldn't melt in his mouth*. I have never understood this expression. It means: *looking innocent*. What that has to do with the temperature of your mouth, I have no idea. And, frankly, if butter wouldn't melt in your mouth, you should call a doctor or an appliance engineer, because either you're very ill, or your fridge is far too cold.

But, anyway, Ryan was looking . . . like that. Although one giveaway that perhaps he wasn't *quite* so innocent was his tie, which, as ever, was not done up properly. It hung loosely, two buttons down from his collar. Ryan liked to think of this as an act of rebellion: his way of saying, "Fine, I'm wearing the tie, but I'm *not* a boy in uniform."

"Right," said Mr Fawcett to Mr Barrington. "But what has all that got to do with what you've got written on your forehead?"

"Pardon, Headmaster?"

"On your forehead, Barrington, you have some words. In black capitals."

Mr Barrington, who had been speaking and waving his arms around quite fast, stopped doing both of these things and looked very confused. He glanced angrily at Ryan before going over to the fireplace in the office, which had a mirror above it.

Mr Barrington looked at his face, confused. He took his enormous glasses off and squinted. Then he put them back on again. Eventually, he said:

"Hm. I can't make out what it says at all. It seems to be saying… (ТИƎЯ ЯOᖷ Ǝ⅃BA⅃IAVA) Is it Russian?"

"Barrington," said Mr Fawcett wearily, "you're looking at it in the mirror."

Mr Barrington looked back at the mirror, even more confused.

"Oh, for goodness' sake, Barrington," said Mr

Fawcett, coming over and standing next to him. "You fell asleep, like you always do, after putting on a dull documentary for Six B to watch. And then Ryan clearly wrote these words on your forehead while you were asleep."

"On his hand, actually, sir," said Ryan.

"Pardon?" said Mr Fawcett.

Ryan walked towards Mr Barrington with something of a swagger, a bit like a master criminal explaining to a not-very-clever detective the details of an ingenious bank robbery he's recently masterminded.

"When Mr B – as you say – falls asleep, he always pushes his glasses up on his forehead. I had to find a way round that. So . . . I wrote it on his *hand* and – well, let's cut a long story short – me and a friend found a way of making him wake up and slap his forehead at the same time."

Mr Fawcett nodded. "I see. So for that to work . . . you must have written it on his hand in mirror writing?"

Ryan smiled politely, like a politician who's being praised but doesn't want to look too pleased about it.

"Headmaster," said Mr Barrington, "I have no idea what this boy is talking about. I certainly was NOT asleep and—"

Mr Fawcett grabbed Mr Barrington's right hand

and held the palm up to the mirror.

"*EMPTY SPACE: AVAILABLE FOR RENT.* It's written right there. *And* on your forehead."

"Oh," said Mr Barrington.

There was a short pause while both men continued to stare into the mirror, and Ryan looked on with amusement.

"Which is *why* Six B were laughing. It's a joke, you see? About you not having a brai—"

"Yes, I understand that, Headmaster. Thank you." Mr Barrington turned furiously to Ryan. "As for you, Ryan Ward, you can take that supercilious smirk off your face right now!" He moved very close to Ryan – who *was*, it has to be said, smirking – and waved a finger very close to his nose. "You won't be smirking when I'm finished with you! Oh no!"

"*Thank you*, Mr Barrington," said Mr Fawcett. "Don't worry. *I'll* deal with this."

Mr Barrington's finger froze, very near the bridge of Ryan's nose. So close, in fact, that Ryan made his eyes go cross-eyed to look at the tip.

But Mr Barrington didn't notice that. Because now it was his turn to smirk, knowing for certain that this meant the boy really was for it.

CHAPTER 5
What I Propose To Do

"So . . ." said Mr Fawcett, after Mr Barrington had left the room with some air of triumph, despite the fact that he *still* had a message on his forehead suggesting he lacked a brain, ". . . good one, Ryan."

Ryan blinked. He'd been expecting a number of things to come out of Mr Fawcett's mouth – insults, threats, punishments – but not compliments.

"No, really," said Mr Fawcett, evidently aware of Ryan's surprise. "Excellent prank. I mean, maybe not up there with that time you let off the fire extinguisher into the dinner lady's pudding tray."

"Only because the stuff that comes out of it looks so much like cream," said Ryan.

"Yes, yes, it does. Doesn't taste like it, though, does it? As at least five children who now will never eat puddings again could tell you. Anyway, as I say, top notch. And then there was that time you got the whole school to *hum* during assembly."

"Very quietly, so you didn't notice it at first . . ."

"Yes. That's the classic method. What else? That butter you spread on the hallway outside the staff room . . ."

"Is Mrs Wang's leg mended now?"

"Not yet. The plague of spiders in the laundry room . . .

"Letting off the fire alarm while everyone was in tears at last year's leavers' assembly . . .

"Telling every child in Reception that Miss Finch was really the Gruffalo . . ."

"She does look a bit like—"

"Oh, I know. That's why it worked so well. And it took two weeks to get them all back to the school without screaming! So. Result. I assume? In your terms . . ."

Ryan frowned. He wasn't quite sure how to react. Mr Fawcett – who normally just gave him a detention without even bothering to hear about whatever new naughty thing he'd done – was behaving very strangely.

But then the headmaster turned to Ryan and said, "So. Taking into account all your naughtiness so far – and adding on this latest bit, the branding of Mr Barrington's forehead – this is what I propose to do."

Ah, thought Ryan. *Here it comes.*

He considered shutting his eyes, as it felt like it was going to be a really big punishment, but then he thought that wouldn't suit his Proud of Being Naughty brand, so he kept them open. To hear Mr Fawcett say . . .

"Resign."

Ryan blinked.

"Sorry?"

"RESIGN."

"Sorry, I'm still not—"

"RESIGN."

Mr Fawcett said it a bit louder this time. Then he said it again. Well, he didn't *say* it. He *sang* it. To the tune of "Football's Coming Home".

"Resign, resign!

Resign, resign!

I'm leaving!

Fawcett's Going Home!"

Although Mr Fawcett was improvising, Ryan was impressed – his words fitted perfectly. He was singing very loudly, and dancing, raising each foot into the air and sticking his thumbs under his armpits, while leaping around Ryan. He continued . . .

"Resign, resign!

Resign, resign!

Free of here!

Far away from YOU!"

The word "you" came with a big point of the finger at Ryan's face. Mr Fawcett stayed pointing into the chorus.

"YOU are off the chart!

Now it's time to get rid!

Thirty years of school

Never seen a worse kid!"

Then he turned to the window, opened his arms and sang louder, more grandly, like an opera singer.

"Resign, resign!

Resign, resign!

I'm off now!

Fawcett's . . . Going . . . Home . . . !"

This last note – on the word *home* – went on for quite some time. And as soon as it was over he skipped – yes, skipped! – across to his desk and starting packing everything on it into his brown-leather briefcase.

Ryan, who had lost some of his cool by now, and whose mouth had been hanging open in amazement, said: "But . . . who's going to be in charge of the school?"

"Ha!" said Mr Fawcett, snapping the briefcase shut. "Maybe *you* should give it a go, Ryan!"

With that he laughed madly, like villains do in pantomimes. And then the head teacher of Bracket Wood School – or possibly the *ex*-head teacher – was gone, slamming the door behind him.

Well, thought Ryan. *That's never happened before.*

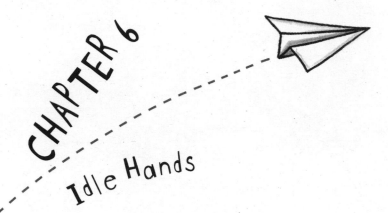

CHAPTER 6
Idle Hands

"**S**o what's he like?" said Ryan's mum, Tina, looking up as she tried to spoon another mouthful of baby food into Holly's mouth. "The new head teacher?"

"I dunno, Mum," said Ryan, hardly taking his eyes off the screen. He was watching, as ever, one of his favourite YouTubers, who was laughing and commenting on internet memes. "He starts tomorrow."

"Oh! So how was school today?"

"Boring."

"That's what you always say."

"Cos that's what it always is."

It was. The same boring lessons, the same boring teachers, the same boring food – meat slop with instant mash carved out of an enormous tray by a dinner lady with an ice-cream scoop. (Ryan always thought this was an insult, teasing you with a serving implement that suggested something nice was coming when it really wasn't.)

Even PE was boring at Bracket Wood. There had been one brief moment of excitement a while back when they had played a posh school called Oakcroft at football and Fred Stone had been amazing, but that was it.

That, really, was why Ryan spent so much time and energy devising pranks. Because it made school a tiny bit less boring.

He went back to clicking keys on his laptop keyboard. Every so often, he took a bite out of the frozen pepperoni pizza next to him. (Not *still* frozen: his mum had cooked it, but it had *been* frozen. I don't quite know why I'm explaining this.)

Tina looked on, worried. She knew that, really,

Ryan should spend a bit less time on the internet. She wasn't sure, in fact, that he should be spending *any* time on it, as she thought he might be watching things not suitable for his age.

But sometimes Tina was so busy that she let her son play on it to keep *him* busy. Idle hands are the devil's workshop, *her* mum used to say, which isn't quite as difficult a saying to understand as the one about butter not melting in the mouth. It means that if people, especially naughty boys, are left on their own with nothing to do, their hands will probably soon start doing naughty things – like ringing people's doorbells and running away, or putting Cup-a-Soup powder in the bathroom shower head. (Which *had* been funny, though Tina did sometimes worry that her laughing quite so much at the sight of her husband's head covered in instant leek and potato may have been one of the reasons he'd left.)

That was always part of the problem. Ryan was

naughty, but sometimes his naughtiness was really funny. Even most of the clips that he watched on the internet – when he showed her – were funny, and rather than telling him off, she ended up laughing with him. It was one of the things she loved about being with Ryan – sometimes it felt more like being with a friend than a son.

But she did worry that although she was always his mum, and sometimes his mate, the one thing she *couldn't* be was his dad – and that he might maybe sometimes need one. Not least to make him do up his school tie properly. By the afternoon, it was always halfway down his shirt. She sometimes wondered if he just pulled it down as soon as he got out of the door.

"Crip! Crip! Crip!" said Holly, pointing at a bag of salt-and-vinegar crisps on the table. Holly in general missed out at least one letter of every word. "Yan!" she continued, to Ryan. "Crip!"

"You won't like those, Holly," said Tina. "They've got a really strong taste. I've heard he's really strict."

Ryan, gathering that his mum was no longer talking about crisps, or to the baby, shrugged.

"Your point is . . . ?"

"Well, Ryan," said Tina, getting up with Holly's bowl, "I think we know what my point is. If the new head teacher is really strict, you might need to watch yourself."

Might I? thought Ryan. *Hmm. A really strict head teacher? That's a bit of a challenge.*

He didn't say that, though. He said, "OK, Mum. I'll be as good as gold." And handed Holly, who was still straining with both arms towards the bag, a salt-and-vinegar crisp. In his defence, her face when she tasted it screwed up in a way that *was* really funny.

CHAPTER 7

I'm. Not. Rubbish.

Ryan's mum, Tina, however, was right.

Mr Carter, the new head teacher, *was* very strict. Perhaps that's the wrong place to stress. Perhaps it should be: Mr Carter, the new head teacher, was *very* strict.

Either way, strictness, in fact, was exactly what the Bracket Wood board of governors had been looking for. OFFHEAD was coming soon and they needed a head who could turn the place round fast. And if that meant dealing with naughtiness – meaning Ryan Ward – with an iron fist, so be it.

All this was pretty clear at the new head's first assembly. As the children filed in, the teachers – Mr Barrington; Miss Gerard, the head of the lower school; Miss Finch, who taught Reception; and PE teacher Mrs Wang, on crutches (she, if you remember, is the one who slipped up on Ryan's butter prank outside the staff room) – were sitting at the back of the tiny school stage.

Then Mr Barrington stood up and said, "Quiet, please!", which he always said, and was always needed, as the noise in the Bracket Wood school hall during assembly was always crazy.

Normally, though, he had to say it about seven times, getting louder each time until he was basically screaming at the top of his voice, his face as red as a tomato. After which he could *finally* take a deep breath and say, "Good morning, everyone!"

and the cross-legged children would reply, "Good morning, Mr Barrington!" or, in Ryan's case, "Good morning, Mr Bummington!"

But on this particular morning he only had to say it once. And everyone, even Ryan, went quiet.

Because *after* he said it once, Mr Carter, who had been facing the wall adjusting his jacket, turned round.

He *did* look like a head teacher – he had short, neat hair and was dressed in a black suit with a black tie (very much done up properly, right to the top button) – but also a tiny bit like a gangster. There was an air of menace about him. His eyes, which were also black, were narrowed and his head was moving slowly round like a searchlight in a prison camp.

Silence.

When he did eventually speak, it was very slowly and deeply. It was as if Batman had walked on to the school stage and said, "Good morning, everybody . . ."

Although, as it turned out, Mr Carter was Scottish. And so far there has not been a Scottish Batman. Having said that, the accent did somehow make his voice even *more* frightening. There was a pause when the whole school seemed too scared to reply.

Mr Carter blinked slowly and then repeated, just a little louder.

"I said, *Good morning, everybody* . . ."

And then, too quickly, falling over each other to say it, the whole school replied:

"Good . . . good . . . morn . . . morning . . . good . . . ing . . . yes . . . good morning . . . morning good . . . Mr Car . . . Mr . . . ter . . . Carter!"

Mr Carter looked into the crowd of children and said, "Yes. Well. We can work on that." He left another long pause. You could almost hear the sound of the children starting to sweat. Then . . .

"This school. It has a reputation, doesn't it? What is that reputation for?"

All the children either looked confused, scared or at the ground. Mr Carter nodded to himself, as if expecting no answer.

"Well, I'll tell you, shall I? *RUBBISHNESS.*" He said this word much louder than the others. Which is why I've written it in capitals. He said it so much louder that some of the Year Ones began to cry.

This didn't seem to worry Mr Carter, who continued: "It has a fine, longstanding reputation for being *rubbish*. It really has won all the awards that don't exist for not being very good. And there's a problem with that, isn't there? Do you know what that problem is, Bracket Wood?"

Apart from the odd Year One sob, silence reigned in the assembly hall.

Miss Gerard, who had very big curly hair, and teeth that always looked a bit like she'd drunk too much red wine the night before – and who was standing just behind Mr Carter – leant over and whispered, "Sorry, Headmaster, are you expecting answers to all these questions? Because I think the children are a little confus—"

"I'll tell you," said Mr Carter as if Miss Gerard wasn't there at all. "It's not you. It's not a problem for you. You can go on being rubbish, and then you can go to a rubbish secondary school and your life can turn out – guess what? – rubbish. That's fine. That's up to you. No. The problem, Bracket Wood, is with me."

He put his hands together in a praying position and placed them in front of his face.

"Because *I'm. Not. Rubbish,*" he said, jutting his hands downwards with each word. "I have turned round every single school I've ever run. Every single school I've ever run has ended up with an OFFHEAD rating of Outstanding. And I'm not going to let *this* school, clearly the worst that I've ever had to work in, tarnish my one hundred per cent reputation. Is that CLEAR?"

Still no one spoke, although at least now there was a response – a lot of children's heads nodded furiously.

"Good. The staff will be pinning notices round

the school this morning with a whole series of new rules that I wish to be followed to the LETTER."

Mr Carter began to leave, then paused and turned his searchlight glare on the assembled children.

"Oh! And one more thing. This school. It also has a bit of a reputation, doesn't it, for *pranks*? It's known all across the land – well, the borough – for being a *no-go zone* for teachers who can't deal with pranks. Fire extinguishers let off into dinner trays, butter spread dangerously on the floor outside the staff room, teachers –" and here Mr Carter glanced round at Mr Barrington – "unwittingly humiliated by words written on their foreheads."

Mr Barrington looked down.

"*Not any more*," said Mr Carter in an icy tone. "If anything like that happens, the perpetrator will be rooted out and punished *immediately* and *severely*. From now on, Bracket Wood School is operating a *zero-tolerance policy* on pranks."

As Mr Carter said this, his eyes seemed to narrow even further and go a shade darker. Like some old portraits, his eyes seemed to stare directly at you wherever you were in the room.

So every child in that assembly hall felt terrified, as if he was speaking specifically to them.

But, if you'd looked very, very closely, you would have realised that Mr Carter was, in fact, staring at and speaking to one pupil in particular – Ryan Ward.

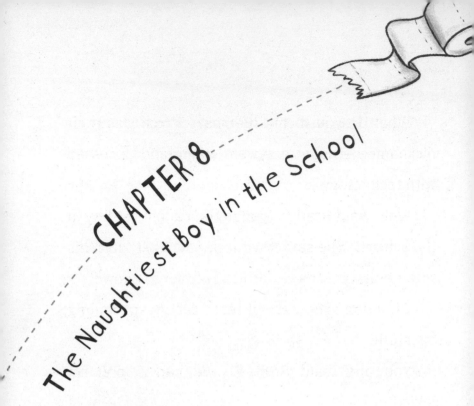

CHAPTER 8
The Naughtiest Boy in the School

"What you gonna do, Ryan? What?" said Stirling.

"Yes, what, Ryan, what?" said Scarlet.

Stirling and Scarlet were brother and sister. They were not in Year Six. They were in Years Three and Two. Most of their time was spent bothering Fred and Ellie Stone about computers and video games, but they bumped into Ryan coming out of assembly and couldn't contain their curiosity.

"What do you mean, iBabies?" Which was their nickname because they were young and obsessed with technology.

"Well," said Scarlet, "you're the naughtiest boy in the school!" She said it without any sense that this was a bad thing, more with a great sense of awe.

"Oh, I don't know about that," said Ryan, smiling bashfully.

"You are," said Stirling. "We had a poll on BuzzyBee."

"That would be some obscure website that no one else has ever heard of?"

"Yes!" said Scarlet.

"So not a very big poll, then?"

"Oh," said Stirling. "I suppose not. Just me and Scarlet and our mum voted. But you won, anyway. You were voted Naughtiest Boy in Bracket Wood History."

"And Best Prankster too!" said Scarlet.

"So . . ." said Dionna, appearing in the corridor

behind them, "if that's the case, Ryan, the new head's thrown you down a challenge and a half, I'd say."

"OK, OK. Well, don't worry . . ." He bent his head down. The others bent theirs too. Ryan lowered his voice. "I'll tell you what I'm going to do—"

"I'm going to tell you what you're *not* going to do, Ryan!" said Mr Barrington. "You're not going to be stopping to have a chat in school corridors any more!"

He raised a piece of paper, which he began to stick to the school notice board with drawing pins. He was doing it with an air of triumph, of "This'll teach you, boy-who-wrote-about-how-I-don't-have-a-brain-on-my-forehead!"

"Because talking in the corridors is *banned* from now on. By order of the new head. All children will move silently from one lesson to the next in a straight line. Failure to do so will lead to immediate detention! As will . . ."

The children gathered round Mr Barrington as he continued to read out the list of new rules, pointing at the piece of paper as he went.

". . . not wearing proper school uniform, so you'd better learn to do up your tie, Ryan."

Ryan glanced down at his tie and shrugged.

"Also," continued Mr Barrington, "arriving one minute late for school, not having a pen or a ruler to hand at all times, persistently turning round in class, persistently making any unnecessary or stupid noise in class and—"

"Thank you for learning all those new rules by heart, Mr Barrington," said Ryan, "as the list is very hard to read upside down."

Ryan walked on.

Mr Barrington turned to the notice board, took his enormous glasses off and then put them back on again . . .

And then pinned the piece of paper the right way up.

CHAPTER 9
Oakcroft

"**N**o, but what *are* you going to do?" said Dionna as they walked home together. Dionna lived a few streets away from Ryan.

"I don't know yet. There's an Open Afternoon for parents next week, isn't there?"

Dionna didn't answer. She was looking away.

"Are you OK?" said Ryan.

"I will be in a minute," said Dionna, tight-lipped, still not looking at him.

Ryan glanced down the road. "Oh," he said. "Oakcroft."

Oakcroft, the grand towers of which Ryan could now see in the distance, was a school that tended to do considerably better in the OFFHEAD reports than Bracket Wood. It was private and mainly attended by children from rich families, except that Dionna, who was not – but who *was* clever – used to go there, having got a scholarship.

She had left, though, halfway through Year Five. Dionna didn't much like to talk about her time at Oakcroft. And she never looked happy when she caught sight of it. Ryan didn't exactly know why, but he was a smart kid and knew that if his friend didn't like to talk about her last school, there was probably a pretty good reason for it.

"Why don't we go another way to your house?" said Ryan, pointing left. "We could avoid the school if we take that road there."

Dionna looked at him now. "But that would mean you having to go miles out of your way."

"Not miles. And it'll give me a chance to tell you what my plan is . . . for the Open Afternoon."

Dionna's face changed from a nervous frown to a thankful smile. "OK! Thanks, Ryan."

They turned a corner and Ryan began.

"So . . . I may need to borrow some stuff from you."

CHAPTER 10
Benny and Bjorn(ita)

"**G**ood afternoon, parents," said Mr Carter.

Even though this was Parents' Open Afternoon, and the point was to make parents feel happy about the school, he said it in more or less the same voice he'd used in assembly, and so most of the mums and dads immediately looked a bit scared.

"Are there any sandwiches?" whispered Eric Stone, father of Ellie and Fred, to his wife, Janine. They were standing in the playground, which Mr Carter had insisted the pupils transform into an inviting space for this special day. It was normally just a long stretch of tarmac with a broken climbing frame at one end, but now there were stalls and colourful bunting, and a big banner that was supposed to say "WELCOME TO BRACKET WOOD PARENTS' OPEN AFTERNOON!"

Although it actually said WELL COME. Which made it sound as if the school was trying to make the parents, who didn't really want to, come. Which in most of the parents' cases – certainly in Eric and Janine's – would be true.

"Bacon ones, maybe?" Eric continued, looking around hopefully.

"No, Eric!" hissed Janine. "It's not a greasy spoon café! It's a school!"

"Thank you all for coming today," continued Mr Carter. "A fair few of you have turned up, which is good. Although I shall be sending letters to those who haven't."

"Blimey," said Tina Ward under her breath, exchanging a glance with Susan Bennett, Barry's mum. "I don't much like *his* attitude!"

"Thank God we made it," said Geoff, Barry's dad.

"It is my intention, as I'm sure your children —" Mr Carter gestured behind him, where Years Two to Six were standing in a series of neat (by Bracket Wood standards) lines — "will have told you by now, to transform this establishment into a school that you can be proud to send your children to."

"And also one that won't get another Inadequate OFFHEAD rating," whispered Jackie Bailey, Malcolm's mother.

"YBBI," said Libby, Malcolm's teenage sister who had been dragged along by her mum and was, as ever, bored. She spoke mainly in acronyms. This one meant *You'd better believe it*.

"Yes!" said Mr Carter. "You HAD better believe it!"

Libby looked a bit shocked that he'd heard. And understood.

"Oh yes, Libby Bailey, I've checked all the files! I know you used to go here, where no doubt you learnt to speak mainly in initials . . . because you didn't learn enough English when you were here, is my opinion!"

"Hey!" said Libby. "TITLU!" Which means *That is totally, like, unfair.*

"But," continued Mr Carter, ignoring her, "that is all going to change. So. We're going to go into the school in a minute, but first, some children from the lower school are going to do a little performance with the school pets."

Two Reception pupils, a girl and a boy, came forward, holding a box. They were followed by Miss Finch, in a very nice dress that made her look like the Gruffalo in a very nice dress, and a smiling Miss Gerard. It was lovely that she was smiling, although this did mean that you could see her teeth, which were particularly red-wine-stained today. Which might have been also why she wasn't walking very steadily.

The children put the box on a table in front of Mr Carter, who grimaced at them in a way that was possibly meant to be friendly and encouraging, but looked more like he was having a small fit.

The girl turned to the parents and, in her loudest outdoor voice, said, "THE SCHOOL PETS ARE TWO TORTOISES. WE GOT THEM FROM ORWELL FARM TO LOOK AFTER."

Then the Reception boy said (but so quietly it was almost impossible to hear) . . .

"Their names are Benny and Bjorn. Which a long, long time ago were the names of two men in the band called ABBA."

"YES!" said the girl, so loudly it made Eric Stone jump. "ABBA!"

"Although the one called Bjorn is actually a girl."

"SHE IS A GIRL!"

"We are going to take them out and talk for a little while about what tortoises eat and how long they live and the best way to look after them."

There was a pause. Miss Gerard, who had been looking off to the side and swaying slightly, went, "Oh!" then came forward and lifted the top off the box.

The loud Reception girl lifted up the male tortoise.

The quiet Reception boy lifted up the female tortoise.

There was a short pause when no one said anything.

Mr Carter frowned.

Miss Gerard went, "Eh?"

Mr Barrington took off his enormous glasses.

And then all the parents and all the pupils –

except the two holding the tortoises, who just looked confused – started to laugh.

Because the male tortoise was wearing a pair of underpants. And the female was wearing knickers. And a bra.

When I say *wearing*, what I mean is that Benny – the male tortoise – had a pair of underpants, classic Y-fronts, size small, draped across his shell. His little legs were actually poking through the holes where legs are meant to go. And Bjorn – the female tortoise – was wearing a pair of flowery knickers in the same way, but above them, across her upper half, there was a small bra, such as might have been worn by a Barbie.

The whole image of the two tortoises wearing underwear was made worse – or better, depending on how you looked at it – by both children deciding to hold the tortoises up, with their bellies facing the laughing parents. I should stress at this point that neither tortoise looked at all bothered by this. Bjorn, in particular, looked quite pleased about the outfit. It made her look more like a lady, more as if her name should be, perhaps, Bjornita.

Mr Carter, however, did not look pleased about it. At all.

"Stop laughing!" he shouted at the children.

They did, immediately.

Mr Carter turned round. "I said . . ." he snarled at

the parents, "STOP LAUGHING." They *also* stopped immediately. You could have heard a pin drop. It looked as if the new head teacher's threatening power had got the situation under control. He turned back to the two Reception children, terrified by now, still holding up the pair of tortoises. They were shaking a little.

Which is possibly why, at that point, Benny's Y-fronts slipped slowly off his little body and fell in a pile beneath him. Bjornita's little head turned to look.

And everyone – parents, children and teachers alike – fell about laughing again.

Everyone, that is, but Mr Carter, who, after looking around with contempt at all the hysteria, picked up the underpants and looked inside the waistband.

"Ryan Ward," he said in a terrifying tone. "My office. Now."

CHAPTER 11

What Punishment?

Ryan Ward looked around the head teacher's office. He had been here many times before, of course. But it had changed. It had only been a week since Mr Carter had taken over, but somehow in that time he'd transformed Mr Fawcett's room – which had always been dusty and untidy, with piles of books and papers everywhere – into a sharp, clean, modern space. The walls, which used to be brown, were now bright white, and gleaming waxed floorboards were visible where previously there had been an old coffee-stained carpet. The depressing grey filing cabinets that used to line the walls were gone, and a new desk, silver and wide and curved, had replaced Mr Fawcett's grotty wooden table with drawers that always stuck.

"I wonder why you chose those particular pants, Ryan?" said Mr Carter, who was sitting on the edge of that desk with one leg on the floor, a bit like a model in a desk catalogue. Next to him on the desk was a pair of pants: the ones that had recently been on Benny the tortoise.

"They were the nearest I had to tortoise-size, sir," said Ryan, who was standing in front of him. "A bit old now, of course. But they did the business perfectly when I was three."

"Hm," said Mr Carter. "I'm not sure I believe you there, Ryan." He reached round and, holding them as far away from himself as he could, picked up the pants. "I think you may have deliberately chosen them because the *name tag* was sewn in to them. A name tag that says –" and he turned the waistband towards him and looked at it disdainfully – "*Ryan Ward.*"

"Well, sir. My mum's a stickler for name tags. Always worrying about me losing stuff."

"Perhaps, Ryan, perhaps. Or perhaps you *wanted* to be caught. Perhaps you *wanted* to be known as the perpetrator of the great tortoises-in-pants prank, the one that *ruined* the new head teacher's Open Afternoon. Because you are proud of being that person."

He held the pants very close to Ryan's face as he said this.

"You know, I like what you've done with this place," said Ryan, pushing the pants down with one finger so he could see over them.

"Pardon?"

"This office. It used to be stuffy and horrible in here. But you've made it all new and flash."

For a second Mr Carter looked genuinely pleased.

"Well, don't think you're going to get round me by praising my sense of interior design, Ryan. But now you mention it, yes, I am happy with what we've done. Still got a few things to clear out from the old head teacher's days – like this . . ." he said, turning back to the desk. He held up a small, very old-looking wooden box. "The builders discovered it under the floorboards when they were redoing the floor."

"What is it?" asked Ryan, not actually very interested, but keen to put off the punishment he knew was coming.

"It's a musical box, though it doesn't actually seem to play any music."

Ryan squinted at the box. On the top was a

weird little symbol, like a circle made out of two curved arrows. Mr Carter opened the box to reveal the mechanism – a series of tiny interlocking gold cogs and wheels – but they remained still and no sound came out.

"Anyway," said Mr Carter, putting the box back down on his desk and speaking in a scary let's-get-on-with-it voice, "I know you're just stalling. So. Ryan."

He took a deep breath and leant towards Ryan.

"You think that me running this school is a challenge to your naughtiness. You think: *I'll show him, this new head teacher with his strictness and his new rules and his frightening manner.* But you're going to have to forget all that. Because I'm shutting you down. Now."

Mr Carter's face was close to Ryan's. *Really* close. Ryan could smell his over-brushed, toothpastey breath. He stayed firm, though, did Ryan. He looked straight back at the new head teacher's fiery black eyes as if to say: *They may be fiery, but the butter is still not melting in my mouth.*

"But what punishment? What will convince you to give up this little campaign I know you're planning? Well, obviously detention. We can do that. That's done. That's in the bank. You're down for five of those this week."

"Yes, sir."

"And obviously a letter home to your mum. Already written. On its way."

"Yes, sir."

"But none of that will really . . . really *pierce* you, will it, Ryan? Really make you wince and think again."

"I don't know."

"I don't know, *sir*." Mr Carter moved away from Ryan, towards the door. "Well, something – or rather someone – you *do* know is *this* person, I think."

He opened the door. Standing in the corridor looking very nervous indeed, was Dionna Baxter.

"In fact, I think she *may* be your best friend . . ."

CHAPTER 12
Even More Frightening

A few seconds later, Dionna was standing next to Ryan in front of the curved silver desk. She glanced at him, fear in her eyes. Ryan half smiled at her, trying to look unbothered, but inside he could feel his tummy dropping like it did sometimes in the car when his mum drove too quickly over a bump.

"I'm right, aren't I, Dionna," said Mr Carter, "that you two are best friends?"

"Um . . ." said Dionna. Mr Carter stared hard at her. She clearly thought better of lying. "Yes."

"And I'm also right in saying that the underwear on the female tortoise was—"

At this point, Mrs Wang walked in. Well, crutched in. Holding up the flowery pants that had been on the female tortoise. With some difficulty.

"—yours?"

Dionna looked down.

"Yeah. Although the bra is technically my sister's. From her favourite Our Generation doll. My parents gave it to her for Christmas. Can I have it back now, actually?"

"We'll see. But I'm glad you've brought up your parents. Because as we know – and I'm sure Ryan knows too – you, Dionna Baxter, only came to us last year from Oakcroft on a *conditional* basis. You were allowed in on the condition that you fitted in well. And, frankly, I think this incident – and your continuing association with Ryan – proves, really, that you DON'T."

Dionna's face crumpled. Her chin started to wobble.

"So," continued Mr Carter, "perhaps I should be writing to your parents and explaining that it hasn't quite worked out for you here. Perhaps it would be better for you to return to your previous school – where I believe your scholarship is still being held open."

"Please, Mr Carter," said Dionna, tears streaming down her cheeks, "I had a terrible time at Oakcroft!"

"Oh, come now," said Mr Carter. "It's an exceptional educational establishment."

Dionna swallowed. "It's not that. It's . . ."

"Yes?"

"Well . . . I was . . . They were . . ." She took a deep breath.

Then looked down, unable to continue.

"They bullied her," said Ryan. "The posh kids

bullied her. You *can't* send her back."

Dionna stared at him.

"How did you kno—"

"I guessed. It wasn't that hard."

"Well, I'm sorry, Dionna," said Mr Carter, who actually did sound a little sorry, but also like it wasn't going to stop him. "I think you should have thought of THAT before you lent your pants to Ryan Ward to put on the school tortoise!"

Normally, this combination of words alone would have made Ryan laugh out loud.

But he didn't laugh. He just looked grimly at Dionna, willing her to stop crying.

He turned back to the new head teacher.

"But, Mr Carter—" he began.

"No *buts*, thank you very much! Your prank ruined our Open Afternoon!"

"It wasn't *her* fault. It was my idea. I just borrowed—"

"It's too late for that now, Ryan," Mr Carter said, turning away.

"No, it isn't!" said Ryan. "It's not fair!" He searched his brain frantically for something that might make the new head teacher reconsider. Then he said, "I don't think Mr Fawcett would have done that! I don't think *any* fair head teacher would do that!"

Mr Carter turned back to Ryan. His eyes narrowed.

"Oh. *Now* you're thinking about poor old Mr Fawcett? Mr Fawcett, who resigned from this school – ran away, in fact, screaming madly, 'I'm free, I tell you, free!' – mainly because of you?"

"Well—"

"You didn't think about what it was like for the poor man while he WAS the head teacher here." Mr Carter shook his head. He walked round to the other side of his desk. "No. You'd never think about that, would you? You'd never think about what it's like to run a place like this! Ha! You know what, Ryan Ward?

I wish – I just wish – that you did know what it's like, what it's really, really like to be a head teacher at a school like this . . . and to have to deal with boys like YOU!"

As he said "YOU", even more loudly than he'd said any of his loud words so far, he brought his fist crashing down on the desk. Which made it even more frightening.

But it also made the musical box, still sitting there, jump up a little, come back down again . . .

And start playing.

MR CARTER

CHAPTER 13
Take Your Pants Back

It was a strange tune, picked out in the eerie, ghost-story plinky-plinky style that all musical boxes play. It was like a nursery rhyme tune, a mix of "Ring a Ring o' Roses" and "London Bridge is Falling Down" and "Three Blind Mice". But with a tiny element of "Let's Marvin Gaye and Get it On" by Charlie Puth, featuring Meghan Trainor.

"That's odd," said Mr Carter, staring at the musical box.

"Yes," said Dionna. "'Let's Marvin Gaye and Get it On'? How can that possibly be the tune? The box is far too old for—"

"No, I mean," he said, "it hasn't been wound up. I doubt it's been wound up for years." He shrugged and turned back to Ryan and Dionna. "Anyway, where were we?"

Neither Ryan nor Dionna wanted to answer that question. But luckily they didn't have to because at that point Mr Carter fainted.

His eyes closed, his knees buckled and he crumpled in a heap on the floor.

"Blimey," said Dionna.

She turned to Ryan, expecting to see him smirking because maybe he'd put something in Mr Carter's tea, or set up some kind of prank that had led to the head teacher fainting.

But Ryan, too, was crumpled in a heap on the floor.

Ryan

Mr Carter

Mr Carter

Ryan

Ryan

Ryan

Mr Carter

Ryan

Ryan

Ryan

Ryan

Mr Carter

Ryan

Ryan

Mr Carter

Mr Carter

RYAN

Ryan

Ryan

Ryan

Mr Carter

Mr Carter

"Oh!" said Dionna. "What's happening?"

"I don't know," said Mrs Wang from where she'd been standing in the corner of the office all along. "But I'd really like you to take your pants back. It's very hard to hold them up when you're on crutches."

CHAPTER 14
Mr Bum Bum Bummington

"Hello? Hello?"

"I think he's waking up."

"Oh, thank goodness! He's been out for over four hours!"

A light flashed in front of Ryan's eyes. He squinted – it hurt. In fact, his whole head hurt.

"Ryan? Ryan? Can you hear me?"

"Yes . . ." he said, with his eyes still closed.

His voice sounded weird. Deeper than usual.

And . . . just *odd*, as if he had a strange accent or something. But he assumed that was a result of . . . whatever had happened. What *had* happened? Last thing he remembered he'd been in the head teacher's office. Then he must have blacked out.

"Ryan? Can you hear me?"

"Yes, I said I can!" said Ryan. He opened his eyes. Staring down at him was a doctor. This was apparent from the fact that she was waving a light in front of his eyes.

Then suddenly next to the doctor Ryan could see Mr Barrington looming above him, eyes magnified by his enormous glasses.

"Ah! Thank goodness! We were worried about you for a while there, Headmaster," said Mr Barrington.

Oh, OK, thought Ryan. *It's a dream. Obviously. It's a dream in which I'm in hospital and Mr Barrington thinks I'm the head teacher. May as well have some fun with that.*

"That's all right, Mr Bummington," said Ryan. "I'm perfectly fine."

"Good, good," said Mr Barrington. There was a pause. He turned back, revealing Miss Gerard next to him.

"Did he call me Mr . . . ?" said Mr Barrington to her quietly.

"Yes. He did," said Miss Gerard. "Must have been just a slip of the tongue. From the bang on the head."

"Yes. I suppose so," said Mr Barrington a bit uncertainly.

"I'm fine, Mr Bum Bum Bummington!" said Ryan. "And don't worry yourself either, Miss Wee-Wee."

"Oh!" said Miss Gerard.

"Clearly quite a bad bang, Miss Wee-Wee. I mean Gerard!" said Mr Barrington.

Mrs Wang appeared, hobbling into his frame of vision. "Ah, I see you're here too, Mrs W—"

"Yes, well, anyway, Headmaster," said Mr

Barrington. "Clearly you're not quite right, but at least you've come round."

"Yes. Good," said Ryan.

"Ryan! Can you hear me?"

That made Ryan sit up. It was the third time someone had called his name from somewhere on the other side of the hospital room. But this time he recognised the voice.

It was his mum's.

He looked over to where it was coming from. Not that surprisingly, he could see his mum sitting beside a bed.

Quite surprisingly, however, the person sleeping in the bed – the person she was speaking to, in fact – was him: Ryan Ward.

CHAPTER 15

AAAAARGGGGGGGGGGHHHHHH!!!!

"Wow. This is a *really* weird dream! Mum! Hey, Mum!" shouted Ryan.

"Hmm. He's calling for his mother," said Mr Barrington.

"Well, at least he's not calling *her* a rude name," said Miss Gerard.

"No, but his mother isn't well, I believe. She's in a home."

It was at this point that Ryan started to worry. Because he'd never had a dream where Mr Barrington had said anything like that. Normally, when Mr Barrington appeared in one of his dreams, he'd be in a clown costume, or have a face that was mainly monkey, and say things like, "You can have the rest of the day off, Ryan!" or sometimes just blow raspberries while jumping up and down for no reason. This felt far too sensible and informative for a dream.

Which meant . . . perhaps it *wasn't* a dream. And now that he'd woken up properly, he had to say that it didn't feel at all like a dream. Everything was really clear and bright and sensible. Well, everything except the fact that over there, in another bed, was another version of him.

"Excuse me," said Ryan. And got up.

"Um, is this all right, Doctor?" said Mrs Wang. "Is he allowed to get up? Also, while I'm here, can you have another look at my leg?"

But the doctor was now at the other bed. The one with Ryan's double in it.

Ryan walked over there. He became aware, as he did so, of feeling taller than normal. He passed Mr Barrington more or less at eye level. Usually those eyes would be glaring down at him through big thick glasses.

He also noticed – because he was, he now realised, wearing one of those hospital gowns that had slits and openings everywhere – that his arms were looking considerably hairier than before. Perhaps *he* had become mainly monkey?

"Hey!" he said when he reached the other bed. His mum was sitting on a chair, holding the hand of the sleeping boy. The doctor was bending over, flashing a beam of light into the other Ryan's eyes with her little torch thing. But he wasn't waking up.

His mother glanced round. Her face looked

very worried and tired. And, on seeing Ryan, quite contemptuous.

"Oh," said Ryan's mum, "I see *you've* woken up, then."

"Yes . . ." said Ryan, very confused. "What's going on here? Who *is* this?"

What was going on with his voice? It sounded not only deeper and gruffer, but also more . . . there was no getting away from this . . . Scottish.

His mum stood up. "Oh, I can't believe this. You were shouting at him and telling him off, or worse, I don't know, and my son comes out of your office having fainted. He's a sensitive soul!"

"He is?" said Ryan.

"Yes! And even worse, now *you* can't even remember who he is!" She pointed to the sleeping figure. "He's Ryan Ward! Six B!"

This made Ryan feel strange. He had only been trying to work out what was going on, but his mum hadn't recognised him – shouting that the boy in the bed was him. It made him feel quite unhappy and a little like crying, actually. In fact, he was just about to cry and say, "No! Mum! *I'm* Ryan!" when Miss Gerard appeared between them.

"I'm sorry, Mrs Ward. Mr Carter is clearly still quite concussed. I'm sure that's the only reason he doesn't remember Ryan. Isn't that right, Headmaster?"

As she spoke, Ryan caught sight of himself in a mirror above the sleeping boy's bed. He saw that the person Miss Gerard was speaking to and, more to the point, the person standing where he was standing, was looking a bit the worse for wear, but also and more significantly, was definitely looking like Mr Carter, the head teacher of Bracket Wood School.

He opened his mouth to scream. But before any words could come out he heard . . .

"AAAAAAAARGGGGGGGGGHHHHHHHHHH!"

He looked down from the mirror. The scream had come out of the sleeping boy's mouth. Because he wasn't sleeping any more. He had woken up.

"AAAAAARGGGGGGH! That's ME! What am I doing over there?"

In that moment, Ryan realised what had happened. He didn't know how or why, but what was clear was . . . he and his head teacher had swapped bodies. He, Ryan, was in Mr Carter's body, and Mr Carter was in Ryan's body. And, frightening and confusing thoughthat was, Ryan also, in that moment, realised something else. He could make this work to his advantage.

Which was why he took a deep breath. And then said to his mum calmly, and now rather relishing the Scottish accent, "Of course, Mrs Ward. I'm so sorry. I have had a nasty bang on the head. But I do obviously recognise Ryan Ward."

The boy's mouth remained open and his eyes staring as Ryan-in-Mr-Carter's-body raised a finger and pointed at him.

"That's him there. I can see him as clearly as I can see in the mirror –" he reversed his pointing finger to direct it squarely at himself – "ME – Mr Carter, the head teacher of Bracket Wood School."

There was a short pause.

Then the boy said, "AAAAA AAAAAAARGGGGG GGGGGHHH! again.

RYAN WARD

CHAPTER 16
No, Yan!

"**B**ut I am. You have to listen. Mrs Ward—"

"Don't call me that again!"

"Well, OK. Tina—"

"Not that either. Mum. That's who I am. *Mum.*"

Two days had passed. Both Ryan and Mr Carter, in their respective swapped bodies, had been discharged from hospital. As far as the doctors were concerned, Mr Carter seemed absolutely fine. Ryan, they felt, was taking a bit longer. He had continued to scream for some time after he'd woken up, particularly when Mr Carter was in his view.

And then, even after the head teacher had been allowed to go, the boy began to claim that it was, in fact, *he* who was Mr Carter, that something terrible had happened and that they needed to call a specialist. The doctors had looked at each other. One of them had said to Tina, "Well, I suppose we could contact the duty psychiatrist?" At which point Tina had said, "Don't be ridiculous! He'll be fine once things get back to normal!" and had taken him home.

But, unfortunately, he wasn't fine. He was *still* saying . . . Well, I'll just continue the conversation from earlier.

"Yes, I understand why you think that you're my mother, Tina, but—"

"*Mum*. Not Tina."

Tina didn't look at him when she said that. She was feeding carrot-coloured mush to Holly.

"'Ocolate. 'Ocolate."

"We haven't got any chocolate. Where are you seeing chocolate?"

Mr Carter screwed up his (now very young) face and took a deep breath.

"The thing is . . . *Mum* . . . I'm not actually your son. I'm not—"

"Yan!" said Holly, pointing at him. "No Yan!" She started to cry.

"Ryan," Tina said, turning to him, "you're upsetting Holly!"

"No Yan!"

Mr Carter stared at the baby, who was still pointing at him through her sobs.

"Well, am I upsetting her? Or maybe, in some sort of primal, pre-cognitive way, she knows that I'm telling the truth, and that I am not Ryan, I am—"

"Ryan! I don't want to hear the words 'I am Mr Carter' again. OK? I don't get this pretending-to-be-the-head-teacher-by-speaking-in-big-words prank, whatever it is. I don't know what you're planning. I'm sure it's very clever and will make everyone at school think you're really great. But I don't care. I've got a lot to think about, I'm tired and I'm simply not interested."

"But—"

"No buts, thank you very much!"

Mr Carter opened his mouth. And then, realising that this was something *he* used to say quite a lot to children, shut it again.

"And eat your vegetables."

"Pardon?"

Tina pointed to his plate. "Eat your vegetables."

Mr Carter looked down. "Um, I don't really like peas."

"Don't be stupid."

"But I don't!"

"'OCOLATE!"

"*Peas* are the only vegetable you *do* like. That's why

I make them for you with everything!"

"Have you got any kale, by any chance? I like that, fried with a touch of garlic."

Tina stared at him. She shook her head, picked up the baby's plate, took it over to the sink and began scrubbing.

"I think that's clean now, Mrs—" began Mr Carter. Tina looked up, daggers in her eyes. "Mum."

She carried on scrubbing. Mr Carter got up from the table and came round to the sink.

"It's just . . . I don't know what to say. I know it seems ridiculous, but I am . . . My name is Michael John Carter. I am forty-three years old. I have been a teacher since I was twenty-two. I specialise in teaching maths and sciences. My first degree is in physics and I have a supplementary degree in education."

"Well, well done, Ryan, for checking out Mr Carter's background on the internet. I'm sure it's all there."

"No, I—"

"Obviously, we all know that there isn't much else to your head teacher than being a head teacher. He does seem very dull and strict."

"Well . . ."

"But when you can tell me something about what Mr Carter is *really* like, as a person — well — then I might begin to listen to whatever it is you're trying to say."

Mr Carter opened his mouth to speak. But then he frowned. He wasn't sure what to say to this. And so, instead, he went back to the table, and began slowly finishing his dinner.

"'Ocolate?" said the baby.

"Ch. Ch. It's Cho-co-late," said Mr Carter, in between mouthfuls of peas.

"'Ocolate?" said the baby.

CHAPTER 17

Ryan →← Mr Carter

Now, as you know, Ryan and Mr Carter have magically swapped places. They've undergone a body swap. So this may become, in the reading, a little confusing. The confusion, I'm hoping, may be sort of fun – I'm going to leave you to work out who's really speaking and who's really thinking.

But as a little rule of thumb: from now on, when I write *Mr Carter*, I mean the person who looks like Mr Carter but is, in fact, Ryan. And when I write *Ryan*, I mean the person who looks like Ryan but is, in fact,

Mr Carter.

I may occasionally remind you who is really who.

Otherwise, best of luck.

Fig. 1: Knowing who's who

Messy hair →

Loose tie ←

Neat hair ↙

Neat tie ←

**Called *Mr Carter*
but it's actually *Ryan***

**Called *Ryan* but it's
actually *Mr Carter***

CHAPTER 18
Small Amendment

"Quiet, please!"

It was assembly once again. Once again it was Mr Barrington who was speaking. Once again, Mrs Wang, Miss Gerard and Miss Finch were seated at the rear of the hall. Once again, Mr Carter had his back to the children, who were sitting cross-legged on the floor.

"Good morning, children!" said Mr Barrington.

"Good morning, Mr Barrington!"

Mr Barrington looked towards the other end of the hall. He saw Ryan Ward sitting there. But he did not hear him say "Bummington". Also, Ryan's tie seemed to be tied right up to his top shirt button. This made Mr Barrington a little confused, though he was pleased his words in the corridor had made a difference.

"I'm sure, school, you'd want to join me in welcoming back our head teacher after his short illness," he continued.

All the children went quiet at this point. None of them looked like they really *did* want to welcome him back.

"I said, I'm *sure* you want to welcome back our head teacher!"

"Welcome back, Mr Carter!" said the children in a not-very-together or enthusiastic way.

At this point, Mr Carter finally turned round. But it was a different turn from the one he'd made in the first assembly of the term, which had been slow and threatening and dramatic.

This turn was quick.

Mr Carter spun on his heel with both arms stuck out and a big grin on his face. It was a bit . . . showbiz. It was as if he was turning to camera in the opening moments of *Mr Carter's Crazy Night Out!* on UKGold. He was wearing the same black suit as ever, although, strangely, the tie was not done up to the top button as per usual, but hanging down loosely, not even properly tied.

"Hey, Bracket Wood!" said Mr Carter. "How you doing?"

Silence. Confusion. Quite a lot of frowning. From both kids and teachers.

"I said . . ." said Mr Carter, "Hey, Bracket Wood! How you doing?"

Still silence, apart from one voice at the back, round about where Ryan was sitting. That voice didn't actually say any words, but it did let out quite a loud groan.

Then the rest of the children said, uncertainly, "How you doing . . . Mr Carter?"

"I'm good! And thank you, by the way, very much indeed, for opening the show here today, Mr Bummington."

All the children laughed. Mr Barrington looked up, *very* confused.

"Let's hear it, in fact, for Mr Bummington!" continued Mr Carter, applauding loudly. The children laughed, and joined in the applause.

"I'm sorry, Mr Carter," said Mr Barrington, approaching him, speaking softly. "I notice you made this mistake in hospital too – it's Barrington. My name. BARRINGton."

"Bummington Barrington?"

"No. Not Bummington Barrington. My first name is Otto."

"I see." Mr Carter paused and looked at Mr Barrington with what seemed to be new eyes. "Really? Otto?"

"Yes."

"What's your middle name?"

"Ernest."

"Right. Got it." He looked back at the audience of children. "Let's hear it for Otto Ernest Barrington!"

The children all carried on laughing.

"Why are they laughing now?" said Mr Barrington to Mrs Wang.

"So!" said Mr Carter. "After my first assembly a whole set of new rules and regulations was outlined. I have a few amendments to make. Miss Finch?"

"Yes?" said Miss Finch, looking terrified – a bit like the Gruffalo, but terrified.

"Don't worry, Miss Finch," said Mr Carter, handing her a sheet of paper. It was the sheet of paper that Mr Barrington had pinned to the notice board in the corridor. "There's no mouse in this forest."

"Pardon?"

"Nothing. Would you mind reading out the new rules, please? One by one?"

Miss Finch looked down. She coughed. Then she began.

"Dress. All children will wear school uniform in neat and respectable condition. Ties must be properly tied."

"OK. As I say, small amendment," said Mr Carter. "All children will wear . . . *whatever they like*! In fact, children who wear the funniest outfits will get the largest amount of praise points! Particular kudos will be given to any child who comes to school wearing a funny hat!"

The staff members sitting behind Mr Carter frowned. But the children, who were warming to this new version of their head teacher, laughed, and some clapped. Meanwhile, Mr Carter ran offstage, which led to even more frowning from the teachers. Then he came back and said, "Perhaps one like this!"

Mr Carter was wearing a top hat. It was one that had been used in the school Christmas play last year to portray the character of Scrooge. And also about four other Victorian characters. Anyway. On the front of the hat was stuck a big photograph of Benny and Bjornita – the tortoises – being held up by the two Reception children, and wearing underwear.

This got a very big laugh from the children. As the laughter was dying down, Mr Carter did an elaborate old-fashioned bow, taking the hat off and waving it across his body.

Then he stood up and said, "Carry on, Miss Finch! Next rule!"

From the back of the hall where Ryan was sitting came another groan.

CHAPTER 19

A Bracketwood Flashmob

Miss Finch looked at Mr Carter open-mouthed. Then she looked back at her piece of paper with the rules on it.

"Right. Um. Well. There shall be NO running in the corridor . . ."

"So again, small amendment," said Mr Carter. "There shall be ONLY running – and shouting and bumping into each other – in the corridor. I want it to be like a constant rugby match out there. Anyone found walking silently, solemnly and slowly to their next lesson will be put in IMMEDIATE detention."

This got a very big cheer from the children.

"Next rule, Finchy!"

"Right . . . well . . . Strict punishment will apply to any pupil persistently turning round in class, or persistently making unnecessary or stupid noises in class."

"Thank you. Well. I'm going to open this one up to the room. What do you reckon we should go for here, guys? Let's have some blue-sky thinking on this."

"All children should turn round in class as much as possible?" shouted Barry Bennett.

"Out of the box, Barry! That's a rule. That's happening. In fact, children will get one praise point per turn. And if anyone manages to spin round as fast as a top while in class, they will earn a bonus ten thousand praise points, which will then be redeemable in the school office for . . . what do we think?"

"Ten pounds!" shouted Malcolm Bailey.

"Cash. Done. Loving your work, Malc!"

"All children shall make as many unnecessary and stupid noises in class as they can?" said Scarlet.

"Now we're cooking with gas! Although don't think – and I can see the staff are worried . . ."

This was true. Mr Barrington, Mrs Wang and Miss Finch were all looking horrified. Even Miss Gerard looked concerned, and usually in assembly she was fast asleep.

". . . that I'm some kind of crazy Lord of Misrule man here. I'm not suggesting that children should be rewarded for just making unnecessary and stupid noises. Heaven forbid."

"Thank the Lord," whispered Mr Barrington to

Mrs Wang. "He's come to his senses."

"No. They've got to be *funny* unnecessary and stupid noises! Like . . . suggestions, please?"

Lots of hands went up. Mr Carter looked around, then pointed. "Fred?"

Fred blew a raspberry. Big laughs.

"Little bit Route One. But still classic. Anyone else? Alfie Moore?"

Alfie did a loud high-pitched woof. Bigger laughs. "Excellent. Works for me. Hey! Morris! Morris Fawcett! Still here even though your dad's gone! What's your poison?

Or should I say, funny noise?"

Morris opened his mouth and made a really loud noise, somewhere between a gargle, a scream, a burp and a yodel. It's hard to capture in letters, but it was something like:

"BRRAACCCGGC CCHHHIIINNN NLLOYYOHOYOY BLAP!"

There was a short silence following this when a few people looked a bit concerned that Morris might be in terrible pain. But then he smiled, as if pleased with himself, and everyone laughed.

"Amazing. You've just landed yourself the ten thousand praise points right there!"

"I thought, Mr Carter, that was for spinning round

like a top in class?" said Miss Finch.

"Oh, Finchy, you're such a stickler!" He turned back to the crowd. "OK! So those are my basic amendments to the rules! There'll be others as we go along, but that'll do for today."

Mr Barrington leant over again to Mrs Wang.

"Thank heavens. Now at least we can get on with the normal school day—"

"It'll do for now because school –" Mr Carter continued, taking some kind of remote control from his pocket – "is cancelled for the rest of the day!"

A huge cheer went up from the hall. Mr Carter pressed the remote control. Immediately, music started to play. It was "Let's Marvin Gaye and Get it On" by Charlie Puth, featuring Meghan Trainor.

"Eh?" said Mr Barrington.

"What?" said Mrs Wang.

"Oh good," said Miss Gerard, who had a bottle of wine still open at home from yesterday.

Mr Carter began dancing, better than you might expect, with some quite cool moves. The children cheered louder than ever. Most of them got up and started dancing too. It was like a Bracket Wood flashmob.

Mr Barrington stood up and tapped Mr Carter on the shoulder.

"Really, Headmaster," he said, close to Mr Carter's ear – which was difficult as Mr Carter's ear kept moving as he danced, which meant Mr Barrington had to dance with him to keep speaking into his ear – "is that wise? Remember we have OFFHEAD coming in a couple of weeks. These new rules are one thing, but just giving the whole school a day off suddenly . . . It won't help anyone, pupils or teachers, get ready for the inspection."

"No, you're absolutely right, Otto," said Mr Carter, twirling round and sticking one arm up in the air, knocking Mr Barrington's glasses off his face.

"Oh!"

"Hey! Everybody!" Mr Carter stopped dancing and pressed the button on his remote control again. The music paused. The children stopped dancing too and looked up. "So Otto has reminded me that we have a situation here – like, an OFFHEAD situation – so because of the impending seriousness of that situation, I'd like everyone to be back at school ready and waiting for lessons tomorrow at nine a.m. sharp! Teachers too."

There was a collective sigh from the children, a sense that this crazy outburst of fun was just a moment and that soon everything would be back to normal.

"Absolutely," said Mr Barrington, although it was quite hard to hear him as he was on his hands and knees with his back to the children, looking for his glasses.

"One small WRINKLE," continued Mr Carter. "I

would like all teachers tomorrow –" he turned to the staff sitting behind him – "all of you lot, and you, Mr Bummington—"

"Barrington!"

"Whatevs . . . to sit in class, at a desk. Basically *be* one of the pupils. And I'd like your place as teachers, in every class, to be taken by some children, hand-selected by you, Miss Gerard . . . from Reception!"

There was a pause. Mr Barrington, still on the ground, shut his eyes. Mrs Wang frowned even more deeply than she had so far. And Miss Gerard said, "What?"

But you couldn't hear any of that because it was drowned out by the sound of every child in assembly cheering.

Well. Every child except one standing at the back. He had stopped groaning, though, and started thinking.

CHAPTER 20
Naughty Bin

Despite not being very interested in the Tudors, Dionna Baxter was enjoying this particular double-period history lesson.

Normally, Mr Barrington wasn't able to make the years 1485–1603 all that interesting, but then again Mr Barrington didn't usually sit on a tiny chair at the front of the class with his legs squashed awkwardly up against the far-too-low-for-him table, looking very uncomfortable indeed.

Nor, normally, did the 6B teacher – today, a four-year-old boy called Caspar – choose to teach the Reformation of the Church and the power struggles in the court of Elizabeth the First while standing on the teacher's desk and singing "The Wheels on the Bus" over and over again.

And just the verse about the babies, at that.

But this was what was happening. Caspar, who was small even for a Reception child and had very blond hair apparently cut by a blind person, had been singing it on repeat ever since the lesson started. In any other context, it might have been really annoying. But in the history class it was hilarious.

Especially being able to see how much it upset Mr Barrington.

"Caspar! Caspar!" said Mr Barrington.

". . . go waah, waah, waah! Waah, waah, waah! Waah, waah, waah!"

"Yes, I've got that. I think we've all got that."

WAAAH!

WAAaH!

"The . . . wheels on the bus . . ."

"What about singing about Henry the Eighth's wives? I'm sure we can do a song about that!"

Dionna laughed. She turned to Ryan, who was sitting next to her. Whom she noticed was not laughing.

"This is so funny, isn't it? Ryan?"

"Yeah," he said. "Ha ha ha ha ha."

Dionna frowned. "Why are you doing that?"

"What?"

"That sarcastic laughing. That laughing that people do when they *don't* think something is funny."

She looked at Ryan. There was something weird about him, had been all morning. He'd hardly said anything, even though school was crazy since Mr Carter had come back from hospital. And now, looking at her, his eyes were also weird. Normally, Ryan's eyes were bright and sparkly and full of fun. Now they looked . . . somewhere between angry and dead. And, most weirdly, his tie was done up! Right to his top button! Like: *OMG?*

"Ha ha ha ha ha," he went. "OK?"

"Please, Caspar," said Mr Barrington, "perhaps you could at least sing something *different*?"

Caspar frowned. Then his face cleared and: "Thhhhhhe . . . wipers on the bus go whoosh, whoosh, whoosh. Whoosh, whoosh, whoosh. Whoosh, whoosh, whoosh . . ."

The class burst into laughter. But Ryan, Dionna

noticed, just looked on, deadpan.

"What's the matter, Ryan? Is it that Mr Carter doing all these funny rules means you can't think of a way of pranking him?"

"No, Dionna. It's not that."

"Because I quite like him now. He seemed like a terrible bloke before."

"No doubt," said Ryan wearily. Which seemed like a particularly odd thing to say.

"Well, what is it, then?"

"Mr Barrington! Mr Barrington!"

"Yes, Caspar?"

"You have do the wipers! Everyone has do the wipers! So you have do the wipers."

"Do I? Really?"

Caspar frowned again. There was a very long pause.

"Yes," he said eventually, "because I is your teacher!"

Mr Barrington sighed heavily. "Whoosh. Whoosh. Whoosh," he said, slowly pointing up his index fingers and moving them from side to side.

"Well, Dionna," said Ryan, after she had stopped laughing, "I'd say it's not actually me who needs to worry about the new head and his crazy rules."

"Sorry, what now?" said Dionna.

"You may perhaps remember that this school has an OFFHEAD inspection upcoming."

"No, Ryan. I did not remember that this school had an OFFHEAD inspection upcoming," said Dionna, doing an impression of his voice, which was still Ryan's voice but with a strangely pompous element added.

"Well, you should. Because *if*, as a result of Mr Carter's –" Ryan's face grimaced as if he didn't quite know how to put his next words – *"odd change of heart* . . . the school gets rated Inadequate again, there is a strong chance *it will be shut down*."

"Oh," said Dionna. Who hadn't thought of that at all.

Ryan nodded. "I see you're starting to understand. Because then you will have to go back to Oakcroft! WON'T YOU?"

He said the last words very loudly. It reminded Dionna, in fact, of the way Mr Carter would suddenly shout words out of nowhere, and how that could be quite frightening.

It was quite frightening for everyone. Even Caspar stopped singing and looked as if he might cry.

With his face still looking like that, he said, "You! Is a naughty boy. You must have bun."

"Pardon?" said Ryan. "A bun?"

Caspar thought for some time.

"*Ishment!*" he said. "You must have bun. *Ishment!* Naughty Step!"

"Right. Thanks," said Ryan, getting up. "Where would that be? I'm not sure there IS a Naughty Step in Six B."

This confused Caspar as there definitely was one in Reception. He looked around. Then his face cleared.

"Over there!" said Caspar, pointing. Ryan followed where his finger was pointing.

"You want me to sit . . . in the bin?"

"Naughty Bin! Naughty Bin! Naughty Bin!"

Something inside Ryan – and when I say something inside Ryan, I mean Mr Carter – sighed.

Because Mr Carter had always been a stickler for the rules whatever those rules were, and Caspar was, at that moment, the teacher, and had told him to go and sit in the bin.

So he did. As his classmates began to clap, laugh and chant, "Naughty Bin!" along with Caspar, Mr Carter-in-Ryan's-body walked over to the bin and plonked himself down on top of some screwed-up coloured paper and half a crayon. To a huge roar from the class.

At least, he thought to himself, *my bottom is a bit smaller than it was, otherwise I'd never have got in.*

Actually, not all his classmates were clapping and laughing and roaring. Dionna Baxter was staring, still frightened, at the floor.

CHAPTER 21
Meowing Like a Cat

This is brilliant! thought Mr Carter (Ryan inside — just checking).

He thought it again and again as he strode through the corridors of Bracket Wood, watching — indeed, dodging — as child after child spun round and round like a top, bumping into other spinning children, while others shouted and screamed whatever came into their minds.

"Poo!" "Bum"! "Willy!" obviously, but some

cleverer things as well – he distinctly heard someone shout "Rat-a-tat-touille!" and someone else, "Nicky nacky noodles!" (I say cleverer – not *much* cleverer.)

Loads of them were wearing funny outfits: some dressed as clowns, some as monkeys, some even as characters from David Walliams's books! Morris Fawcett had gone for the funny hat option, with a hilarious photo from the internet stuck to it of a cat eating a banana, and Mr Carter was kind enough to turn it round the right way as he passed.

He went round a corner. More crazed children ran past, bumping into him and each other, and shouting. It made him laugh. Most of them disappeared at that point into classrooms. Except for one, who bumped into him. Who wasn't, in fact, a kid. It was Miss Gerard.

"Oh, sorry, Miss Gerard!" said Mr Carter.

"Thatsh OK, Headmaster," said Miss Gerard. Well, she didn't say it. It was more of a slur, really. Her teeth were very black today, Mr Carter noticed.

He also noticed that she didn't back away. In fact, if anything, she was still bumping into him long after she didn't have to bump into him any more. Her face was way too close to his.

"I have to shay, Head . . . Whatsh your firsht name again?"

"Er . . ." Mr Carter realised he didn't actually know this. So he guessed, thinking of the first name that came into his head. "Gerard," he said.

"Yesh, that's me," said Miss Gerard. "But whatsh *your* name?"

"No," said Mr Carter, thinking that maybe this wasn't a very good idea, but feeling that it was too late to change it now. "My first name is . . . Gerard."

"Oh!" said Miss Gerard. "That's amayshing!" She looked at him slyly, reaching out a hand and, for some reason that Mr Carter couldn't fathom, stroking the lapel of his jacket with one finger. "If we were married, you'd be Gerard Gerard."

Mr Carter didn't know much about marriage, coming as he – Ryan – did from a broken home himself, but he knew that didn't sound quite right. He didn't get a chance to say so, though, because Miss Gerard laughed a lot at this remark, showing her very black teeth as she did so. Mr Carter didn't know what to do, so he joined in the laughing, feeling a bit uncomfortable.

"Anyway, Gerard," she said, suddenly looking very serious and frowning, "I just wanted to shay I think it's amayshing what you're doing to this school. Shayking it up. Trying someshing new. Itch great. Unushall."

"Er, thanks."

The stroking finger had now crept up to his ear. She was tickling his earlobe. It felt really, really weird.

"So. Gerard. If you fanshy going out shumtime to talk about your plansh in a bit more . . . *detail* . . . then jusht . . ." She mimed making a phone call with her other hand – very, very badly.

"Oh, right. OK."

"I'm very good with *details* . . ." she said. And winked.

"Right," said Mr Carter. She was very close to him now. Her breath smelt – well, like her teeth looked – like she'd drunk a lot of red wine, perhaps a bit more recently than just the night before. "Are you . . . OK, Miss Gerard?"

"Oh yesh! I feel fantastic! Your speech in there – well, it made me want to shelebrate. So I did. I went out and had a tiny shelebration at the pub across the road. It'sh not just the kidz you want being wild and crazshy, ish it?"

Mr Carter frowned. He hadn't really thought about how his words might have inspired any of the teachers. He had to think about it now, though, as Miss Gerard suddenly started spinning like a top with her arms out and meowing like a cat.

Mr Carter ducked. But not quickly enough to stop Miss Gerard falling on him and laughing hysterically. She ended up squashing his face down on the floor.

"Oh! Mr Carter!" she squealed through her laughter. "I didn't mean *that* crazshy!"

He managed to squeeze himself out from under her and she blinked up at him.

"So what do you think, Gerry? Can I call you Gerry? Fanshy going over the *detail* any time soon?"

"Um . . ." he said. He could feel himself starting to sweat, a weird feeling, as it involved him starting to smell in ways that he was not used to. And then, thank the Lord – or, rather, his own new rules – he heard a huge roar of noise from a classroom nearby.

"Er . . . as the head teacher, Miss Gerard, I REALLY need to go and find out what that is! Bye!"

And he rushed towards the door. Miss Gerard remained on the floor. Very slowly, her eyes closed.

CHAPTER 22
Time for the Next Lesson

The roar that Mr Carter had heard was the roar of 6B enjoying Ryan getting into the bin. By the time he opened the door, though, Caspar seemed to have forgotten Ryan was there, and had begun drawing a series of houses on the board, all of which had a sun that looked a bit like a big spider above them.

"Hey!" said Mr Carter.

Everyone looked round. Behind him, one or two

pupils frowned at the sight of Miss Gerard stretched out on the corridor floor, snoring.

"Good morning, Mr Carter!" said the rest of them.

"Hello, my favourite form!" he said. "What's going on? Oh! I see Caspar's doing some brill teaching – good on you, Cas!"

"Thuuuuhhh horn on the bus goes—"

"Beep, beep, beep. It does. It so does." His eyes scanned the classroom. They settled for a moment – or so it seemed to her – on Dionna. In fact, it seemed as if Mr Carter was *smiling* at her. She looked round in case she was mistaken and he'd meant the smile for someone behind her. Which was a bit silly, as I have already explained that she and Ryan sat at the back of the class.

Either way, when she looked back, Mr Carter was no longer smiling at her. He was looking around at the rest of the class.

"Now. We are missing someone, aren't we? In Six B.

Where is he? Where oh where is . . . Ryan Ward? It's odd. It seems as if he's vanished. As if he's gone completely! Absolutely cannot be found in his normal place."

"Here I am," said Ryan Ward in a weary voice.

Mr Carter turned round, then laughed.

"Oh! *That's* where you are. In the bin! What are you doing there?"

Ryan stared at him, a very *You saw me as soon as you came in – why are we bothering to pretend otherwise?* look on his face. "Well, *Head Teacher* . . ." His voice landed on those words heavily. "I think what happened was that even Caspar, a four-year-old, could see that I –" and here his stare at Mr Carter grew harder – "*Ryan Ward*, was – how can I put this? – trash. Yes. That's the right word: *trash*. He looked at me, *Ryan Ward*, and thought about *Ryan Ward's* behaviour, and clearly felt there was only one place for me – *Ryan Ward*." He turned his fierce gaze to Caspar. "Isn't that right, sir?"

Caspar seemed at a bit of a loss as to what to say. So he said, "Shh. Shh. Shh?"

"That's what the mummies say, yes," said Ryan.

"And," said Mr Carter, who seemed a little shaken by Ryan's speech, "I think it's a good thing to say to you . . . *Ryan*. Perhaps shushing you is a good idea. Because, frankly, I think you . . . well, I think you may have some self-esteem issues."

"Do you," said Ryan. Not with a question mark.

"I do. Here," said Mr Carter, extending a hand, "let me help you out of that."

Ryan stared at him again. "No thanks. I can get myself out."

And he did easily enough and walked back to his seat.

There was a tense silence following this exchange. But then Mr Carter seemed to recover his energy and beamed at the class.

"Right! That's that sorted. Now, I know Caspar's

been doing a brilliant job with History, but it's time for the next lesson: PE!"

Everyone in the class looked at each other. Mr Barrington – with some difficulty and what appeared to be quite a lot of pain – uncurled himself from the small chair and too-low table. It was a much slower and more awkward process than Ryan climbing from the bin. He stuck both legs out to the right and then pushed himself out, sliding completely to the ground, then kneeling, going "uggh" a lot, before heaving himself up and brushing himself down.

"Excuse me, Mr Carter," he said, after breathing heavily for a bit. "You may have forgotten – we only do PE on a Wednesday afternoon."

"Oh yes, I did forget. Hang on a minute, let me check my timetable."

Mr Carter took out a piece of paper from his pocket. He looked at it for a moment, concentrating. Then he said, "Hmm. But this says . . ."

He turned it round to face Mr Barrington and the class. On it was written in block capitals,

BUM OFF, BUMMINGTON!

Which got a very big laugh from the classroom.

"Oh," said Mr Barrington.

"Everyone to the playground!" said Mr Carter.

CHAPTER 23

The How to Be a Head Teacher Handbook

The whole school was standing in the playground. By *the whole school* I mean every single pupil. And by *standing in the playground* I mean standing at one end of the playground. At the other were the teachers. In the middle was Mr Carter. With a referee's whistle round his neck.

"Right!" shouted Mr Carter. "It's time to play . . . British Bulldog!"

"Oh dear," said Mrs Wang.

"I thought it might be," said Miss Finch.

"Hooray!" said Miss Gerard, and fell over.

"Teachers versus pupils, obviously!" shouted Mr Carter.

The teachers – who were severely outnumbered – gulped.

"You know the rules! Each side has to get as many people to the other end as possible! And each side has to try to stop the other side doing that! By any means NECESSARY!"

"Excuse me," said Mr Barrington.

"Yes, Bu—"

"Don't call me Bummington! Please!"

"Oh, OK."

"Is that fair, sir? There are a *lot* more of them."

"Yes, but you're bigger."

"Well . . ." said Mr Barrington uncertainly, looking over at the older children, some of whom were stretching and limbering up in anticipation. "I don't know about that."

"The Gruffalo certainly is."

"Who's he talking about?" said Miss Finch.

"But hey!" said Mr Carter. "I've thought about that. I've come up with a way of making this game of British Bulldog a bit different! Which might help!"

He put the silver whistle hanging round his neck in his mouth and blew loudly. At which point, Scarlet and Stirling suddenly appeared, one on each side of the playground. Stirling stood in front of the teachers holding a box. Scarlet stood in front of the children with a similar box.

"iBabies – I mean Scarlet! Stirling! Thank you for your help! Now, here's how this works. When the boxes are open, something will come out of each one. That thing is your captain: your *leader*. No one is allowed to go further ahead than that thing. All team members must stay behind the thing. OK?"

Everyone – teachers and pupils – frowned. But

Mr Carter raised his arm.

"The game begins on the whistle, at which point Scarlet and Stirling will open their boxes. So . . . !"

He blew hard on his whistle.

Stirling opened his box. Out of which came Benny the tortoise. Scarlet opened her box. Out of which came Bjornita the tortoise.

Benny stood still. Bjornita stuck her long neck out, looked around and very, very slowly moved forward.

"Come on, teams!" shouted Mr Carter. "Go for it! British Tortoise!"

"Go for what?" shouted Ellie Stone.

"Follow your captain! In fact, make like your captain!"

With that, Mr Carter started doing an impression of a tortoise. He bent over low, stuck both his arms out crookedly and moved in slow motion while sticking his head up and looking around as if for pieces of manky lettuce.

Everyone looked on, amazed. It was, it has to be said, not an action most people – pupils and teachers – would have found in the *How to Be a Head Teacher* handbook. If such a book exists.

"Come on!" he shouted in a deep, croaky voice, meant, one would have to assume, to be tortoise-like.

And gradually the children – Barry Bennett, Jake, Lukas and Taj, Ellie and Fred Stone, Isla and Morris Fawcett, Scarlet and Stirling, and Malcolm Bailey (who seemed, for some reason, particularly good at it) – all started to copy him and walk like a tortoise.

"Come on, teachers! Hey!" said Mr Carter, now on all fours. "Tortoise towards the other side! Or you'll lose!"

Mr Barrington looked at Miss Finch, who looked at Miss Gerard, who looked at Mrs Wang, who shrugged, put her face down, stuck her crutches out

and started tortoising behind Bjornita towards the tortoising children. It worked well, actually, because tortoises move a little bit like they are on crutches all the time.

CHAPTER 24
My Name Isn't Doreen

An hour later, it was time for lunch. Nobody had really won British Tortoise – Benny had wandered off the playground towards the patchy grass side area, in search of . . . patchy grass, basically . . . which meant that the kids' team had to follow him there. Then Bjornita had been frightened by all the noise and just retreated into her shell, which meant the teachers had to curl up into little balls with their hands over their heads at the other end of the playground. But it had been funny, and everyone – even maybe Mr Barrington – had kind of enjoyed it.

In the lunch hall, the dinner ladies were lined up with their silver trays and big spoons as usual. The children were all waiting to get their food as usual. *Un*usually, though, Mr Carter was standing in front of the dinner ladies, dressed as a chef – a proper posh old-style French one with a tall white hat and an apron and an enormous spoon.

"OK! Good work out there on the playground!"

"Who won, Mr Carter?" shouted Alfie Moore. "The kids or the teachers?"

"Hmm. I'd say the tortoises. But now I know you will have built up an appetite. So I want you to enjoy your lunch. And in particular some small changes I've made to your lunch options!"

This led to a buzz of chatter around the hall.

"Morris! What day is it?" Mr Carter continued.

"Er . . ."

"Fair enough. Barry?"

"Monday!"

"Correct! And what's on the menu on Monday?"

"Stew and mash."

A groan mixed with an "*urrrgh*" went round the hall.

"Not entirely correct. Or, at least, I would say that on the menu on Monday is not stew and mash, but . . . poo and mash!"

A very big laugh went round the hall. Particularly Years One, Two and Three, for whom anything to do with poo and wee made them go mad with laughter.

"So . . ." Mr Carter turned to one of the dinner ladies, a very stout one with a brick of grey hair covered in a plastic net. "If you don't mind, Doreen . . ."

"My name isn't Doreen. It's Lisa."

"Right. Sorry."

"You just gave me a name that sounds like a dinner lady."

"I did. You're absolutely right. So, Lisa . . . could you uncover today's main course?"

Lisa nodded to herself and then with a tiny bit of a flourish placed her hand on the top of her stainless-steel cover and lifted it to reveal:

"Stew!"

A groan of disappointment went round the room.

"Ah. But what *kind* of stew is it, Lisa?" Mr Carter held up the tray. "Let me give you a clue. What's the best thing about cake? Particularly when you or your mum – or dad, no sexism here, please – are *making* a cake? Anyone? Sam Green, you've eaten a few cakes . . . ?"

"Er, the mix?"

Mr Carter put his index finger on his nose and pointed at Sam with his other index finger. Which meant that Sam had got it right. He then twirled that finger round and flicked it through the food in the tray. Which was, as it turned out . . .

"Cake-mix stew!"

All the children in the hall cheered. Mr Carter lifted his finger coated with cake-mix stew high in the air, threw his head back and opened his mouth wide. And then dived his finger into his mouth.

"MMMMM!" he said, slurping it out again. "Delish! And to go with it?"

Lisa lifted the top of the other stainless-steel container in front of her.

"Mash!"

"What kind of mash, though?"

Lisa lifted her ice-cream scoop.

"Ice-cream mash! Which is basically just ice cream! In the potato tray!"

"I always hoped those ice-cream scoops would one day be used for the real thing!" said Mr Carter. He turned to another dinner lady standing further down the serving table.

"And for dessert . . . Doreen?"

"My name isn't Doreen either. It's L'Shaniqua!"

"Sorry, L'Shaniqua."

"Well, it's quite hard to think of a dessert that *can* really follow cake-mix stew and ice-cream mash."

"You'd think so, wouldn't you? But . . ."

"But you've insisted. So it's just –" she removed the top of her container with slightly less of a flourish than Lisa – "sweets. Loads of sweets. Every sweet you can think of!"

"Including sour sweets?" queried Barry Bennett.

"Oh yes, Barry," said Mr Carter. "Including Haribo Tangfastics."

And it was, indeed, a huge tray of sweets, all still in their wrappers: Twixes and Mars bars and Boosts and Aeros and Airwaves and Chomps and Buttons and Juicy Fruits and, yes, Haribo Tangfastics, and Topics and Flakes and Drumsticks and Starbursts and Toffee Crisps and Curly Wurlys and Double Deckers and Smarties and Bountys even though no one likes them.

That was it. There was the hugest cheer so far from the dining hall, and all the Bracket Wood pupils charged towards their lunch in a way that no teacher had ever seen before. There was a scramble for the sweets with lots of children falling over each other as they went for dessert first. It became a massive free-for-all, with no one even waiting for the dinner ladies to serve anything. Every pair of hands was just grabbing at what they could.

"STOP!" shouted a voice very loudly.

And the voice was so commanding, so grown-up-sounding, even though it clearly belonged to a child that, amazingly, everyone did.

CHAPTER 25

OH! HEADMASTER CAR-TER!

Everyone stopped grabbing sweets and looked round. At the back of the dining hall, one child had stood on a chair. It was Ryan Ward.

"Just stop!" he continued, still sounding very grown-up. He sounded, to use quite a long and difficult word, very authoritative (like someone in authority – to make it a series of slightly smaller words). "It's bad enough that you're all going to eat this food. None of which is approved by Jamie Oliver!"

A number of pupils and teachers frowned at this thought. Miss Gerard even woke up.

"But if you ARE going to eat this *junk* then at least can we form a proper queue!"

Now *everyone* frowned. Especially Dionna. Who, while still frowning, said, "Ryan? Are you OK?"

He didn't answer her. But she felt worried. He had been behaving so weirdly since coming back from hospital. And now his voice, even though it was definitely his voice, didn't sound like him at all.

"Yes. Good question, Dionna," said Mr Carter. (He was the only one who *wasn't* actually frowning.) "Are you OK?"

"Yes, *Mr Carter*," said Ryan, staring at him. He spoke calmly and slowly and made the words "*Mr Carter*" – much like in the lesson that morning he had made the words "*head teacher*" – sound sarcastic. "I'm *fine*."

"Are you?" said Mr Carter. "Because I think it's

perfectly fine the way lunch is going at the moment. I think everyone scrambling over each other and fighting for sweets is fun. You're all enjoying it, aren't you?" he added, turning to the pupils.

"Yes!" said Morris Fawcett. Well, he actually said, "Ysbz!" because his mouth was already full of Topic.

"OK! So, relax, Ryan!" Mr Carter went over to him. "Chill! Take a load off! Skrillax! Wind down! Loosen your goose!"

Now everyone moved their frowns towards Mr Carter. Dionna thought, *Never mind Ryan not sounding like himself, who is Mr Carter sounding like now?*

"Right . . . well, that's *very* head-teacherly talk, isn't it?" said Ryan. He was still standing on the chair so his eyes were at the same level as the head teacher's. In fact, they may have been higher. For a second, at least from Dionna's point of view, it looked like Ryan was the adult and Mr Carter was the child. "Odd, this, isn't it? The pupil talking properly; the head teacher using stupid slang."

"Hey! I was using it ironically. I'd never actually say *skrillax* seriously!"

"But odder still," said Ryan, looking around, "is this whole situation. A head teacher changing the lunch menu to sweets and a pupil complaining about it. A head teacher saying, 'Hey, let's just have a free-for-all,' and a pupil saying, 'No, I think everyone should queue up quietly and properly.'

What *is* going on? What does everyone here *think* is going on?"

The pupils looked at each other. A few murmurs of "It *is* a bit odd . . ." and "Yeah, that is kind of upside-down from normal . . ." were heard. Alongside one of, "Yum, I love Topics."

Mr Carter looked over his shoulder at the dining hall. For a second, a cloud of doubt passed across his face, as if Ryan pointing out the strangeness of the whole thing had thrown him. But then he turned back to Ryan, smiled and said, "Not just any pupil, Ryan. The *naughtiest* pupil in the school. And the naughtiest pupil in the school would *always* go up against the head teacher. Wouldn't they? Even if the head teacher was doing something fun and crazy and that *most* kids would like. Even if I gave the whole school the day off after lunch . . . which maybe I will!"

"Don't do that!" Ryan shouted.

"You see?" said Mr Carter to the watching children. Some of them were staring at Ryan now. And not in a good way. "Or if I said that no one has to come in tomorrow either . . ."

"That would be ridiculous!" shouted Ryan.

"No, it wouldn't!" shouted Malcolm Bailey.

"It would be great!" shouted Sam Green.

"We could stay at home and play on our ZX27s all day!" shouted Stirling.

"An obscure type of old computer that only plays a tennis game from the 1970s!" shouted Scarlet.

"You can't just cancel school for a day and a half!" said Ryan desperately.

"I can and just did!" bellowed Mr Carter, turning to the rest of the dining hall with both arms in the air like he'd just scored a goal. All the children cheered.

"And now I'm cancelling HOMEWORK! FOREVER!"

An even bigger, happier cheer went up. And then Morris Fawcett started a chant to the tune of a song called "Seven Nation Army" by a band named the White Stripes. Morris wasn't a fan of the White Stripes, but he'd heard people chant the name of some politician to this tune on TV and he thought it sounded good. It went . . .

"OH! HEADMASTER CAR-TER! OH! HEADMASTER CAR-TER!"

Immediately, everyone joined in because of course everyone was very happy about Mr Carter's latest ruling.

"Oh no, really," said Mr Carter. "No need."

"OH! HEADMASTER CAR-TER! OH! HEADMASTER CAR-TER!" went the whole dining hall, with most of them pointing at Mr Carter in time with the chant. Except for the Reception to Year Two children, who had no idea what was going on.

As the song continued, Ryan seemed to shrink a little. His eye level came back down in line with Mr Carter's, who looked at him sympathetically.

"It's confusing, isn't it, Ryan?" said Mr Carter. "Because now *I'm* the one being naughty. And so for you to carry on fighting me, *you've* got to become a goody two-shoes. Which is just a bit sad for you, I imagine."

"No! That isn't what's happening. I'm—"

"Just stop it, Ryan!" went a shout.

"Yeah, give it up, Ryan!" went another.

"Leave Mr Carter alone, Ryan!"

"It's not really a tennis game. I mean there's no rackets, just little walls that move up and down!"

"OH! HEADMASTER CAR-TER!"

Ryan looked around. The pupils who weren't chanting had sat down and were tucking in happily to cake-mix stew with ice-cream mash (and a side plate of confectionery for dessert). Mr Carter was joining in the chant about himself, jabbing his hands in the air in time with it, and some of the stronger and larger 6B boys were trying to lift him on to their shoulders.

Through the windows that looked out on to the corridor, Ryan could see some other children who had decided to act immediately on Mr Carter's promise of a day off. They were running and shouting and spinning down the corridor in accordance with the rules as they barged each other towards the exit. At least three were wearing funny hats. On the other side, in the playground, he could see the two tortoises wandering around, not having been put back into their pen.

Above the sound of the chanting and the running and the munching, he thought he could hear Caspar still singing "The Wheels on the Bus" as a teaching method for some class somewhere.

Oh well, thought Ryan (just a quick reminder: I mean Mr Carter in Ryan's body), *at least it can't get any worse*.

At which point he heard something else.

"EXCUSE ME!" said a voice very loudly.

"CAN ANYONE TELL ME WHERE TO FIND THE HEAD TEACHER?"

At the door stood two people, a man and a woman. The man, who spoke with quite a strong northern accent, was bald with a moustache, and the woman was Indian with long straight dark hair. He was holding a briefcase, she a notebook.

"Who wants to know?" asked Mr Carter.

"I AM MR MANN. THIS IS MY COLLEAGUE, MISS MALIK. WE ARE INSPECTORS. FROM OFFHEAD."

"Oh! Head teacher Car—" went the chant.

Before stopping.

For a very long time.

Until, finally, Morris Fawcett went, "—ter."

CHAPTER 26
This is Getting Weird

The hastily convened meeting between Mr Carter (Ryan, in reality – OK, I think we're good) and the OFFHEAD inspectors that followed lunch cannot be said to have gone particularly well.

Mr Carter had begun by trying to be . . . well . . . like the real Mr Carter. It didn't last very long.

"So I know it looks . . . um . . . not too good right now at this . . . establishment, but I promise you, Mr Mann . . . Sorry, is that *really* your name?"

"Yes," said Mr Mann, frowning. He was sitting opposite Mr Carter's desk. Miss Malik was next to him.

"As in . . . like . . . Mister Man?"

"Brian Mann is my name, yes. As I've said."

"So which one are you?"

Mr Mann frowned a bit more, and exchanged a glance with Miss Malik.

"I'm Mr Mann, and this is Miss Malik. As I thought I made clear, already . . ."

"No," said Mr Carter, "I mean, which Mr Man are you? Mr Muddle? Mr Worry? Mr Wobbly-Tickle?"

"Mr Carter . . ." said Miss Malik.

"No, that's me. Well, sort of," said Mr Carter.

"I'm sure that's very amusing, but we need to talk about the state of this school."

"Right, right."

"It's *in* one," said Mr Mann grimly.

"Yes. I see what you're saying."

"A state," he said even more grimly.

"Yes, I get it. Honestly," said Mr Carter. "Don't spell out your jokes, Mr Mann. Didn't Mr Funny ever tell you that?"

Mr Mann looked more confused than ever.

"It is, though, to be fair," said Mr Carter, "a *state* school. So." He poked Mr Mann in the arm with his finger. "Eh? D'you see? HA! HA! HA! HA! HA!"

Mr Carter's laugh didn't seem to be a real laugh, but an ironic one – one that was making fun, in other words, of Mr Mann's joke about the school being in a state. Which hadn't actually been a joke.

Mr Mann looked at Miss Malik, who shrugged. Mr Mann opened his briefcase and took out a wodge of papers.

"OK, well. I was hoping we weren't going to have to do this, but I am afraid that we have to report back on our findings to OFFHEAD. And I'm pretty sure that, based on those findings, they will give

Bracket Wood a rating of Inadequate. Which will mean, given how badly the school has performed in the past, an immediate clos—"

"Ahem."

Mr Mann, Miss Malik and Mr Carter all looked round. The person saying "Ahem" – he was *actually saying* the word "ahem", not coughing – was Ryan Ward. He was standing at the door to Mr Carter's office.

"Excuse me, Mr Mann, Miss Malik . . ."

"Yes?"

"Could I have a word?"

Mr Mann turned to Mr Carter. "Do you normally let pupils just walk in here and interrupt meetings whenever they like?"

Mr Carter shrugged. Mainly because he was keen to know what Ryan was going to say.

"Hmm," said Mr Mann with a glance at Miss Malik, "I suppose nothing would surprise me about this school and the attitude of its head teacher any more."

"Rude," said Mr Carter. "Talking about me like I'm not here."

"I do apologise for interrupting," said Ryan, walking in, "but I thought perhaps you should know that Mr Carter isn't actually very well at the moment."

"What?" said Mr Carter.

"As you will discover if you check the local hospital records, Mr Carter unfortunately had a very bad fall recently and had to be hospitalised after being knocked unconscious. Since he came back to the school, he hasn't quite . . . been himself," continued Ryan.

"Don't be crazy!" said Mr Carter. "I have totally been myself! I have been so like myself I'm not even joking!"

Ryan made a *There you are!* glance at the OFFHEAD inspectors. Who looked at each other with raised

eyebrows. Miss Malik put her notebook down and rummaged in her bag.

Mr Carter got up from behind the desk. "Oh right, I see you're starting to believe him! Well, what you need to know about this pupil – Ryan Ward – is that he's the naughtiest boy in the school! So! He probably would say just *anything* – including making everyone think the head's gone oops-upside-*his*-head – for a prank!"

"It's true," said Miss Malik, looking at her phone. "We have access to hospital records and, yes, he was admitted for concussion last week."

"Can you please stop talking about me like I'm not here?" said Mr Carter.

"Well, you *aren't* here!" said Ryan Ward. And then, pointing to himself, "You're *here*!"

"OK," said Mr Mann, getting up and closing his briefcase. "This is getting weird."

"I agree," said Miss Malik, standing as well.

"So look," said Mr Mann. "I have no idea whether what this boy says is true, but clearly, Mr Carter, you have been unwell. We at OFFHEAD are nothing if not fair and so we will delay our rating of the school." And here Mr Mann glanced at Miss Malik. She glanced down at her notebook, then back up at him and nodded as if confirming something unsaid.

"For a week. Just one week. This is something we do in unusual circumstances. So you as the head teacher of this school have one week to put your house in order."

"And," said Miss Malik, "do try not to just get it back to its usual . . ." She searched for the appropriate word.

"Rubbishness?" offered Mr Carter.

"Yes, I suppose. Its usual rubbish standard. What we need to see, if Bracket Wood *is* not going to be closed down, is concrete evidence of radical improvement."

"So," said Mr Mann, "you need to prove yourself a grown-up, Mr Carter. You're at the bottom now, but your slate can be wiped clean!"

Mr Carter sniggered as if he was trying not to.

"What are you laughing at?" said Miss Malik.

"Sorry," said Mr Carter, still sniggering, and then

he pointed a finger at Mr Mann. "He said 'wipe' and 'bottom' in the same sentence." Mr Carter's snigger became a full-blown laugh as he *stopped* trying to suppress it. Mr Mann frowned, Miss Malik shook her head and then both of them made for the door.

"One week!" said Mr Mann as he went.

"Best of luck," said Miss Malik to Ryan Ward. She didn't, in all honesty, sound very hopeful.

CHAPTER 27
All Fourteen Varieties

After the OFFHEAD inspectors had left, Mr Carter smiled, shook his head and sat down behind the head teacher's gleaming new silver desk. "It's very weird, isn't it, Mr Carter?"

"Well," said Ryan, "finally we agree on something! OK. So . . ." He came over to the desk. "Look. You've had some fun. You've had your little laughs at my expense. You've made the school into a wacky and crazy place for your friends. Obviously, now that

OFFHEAD have turned up and the whole school is under threat, we need to stop this. But I'm prepared, unusually for me, to let it all go. No punishments. Once we're back in our normal bodies, of course."

Mr Carter nodded as if he agreed, as if clearly this was the only way to go. But then, without pausing the movement, his head went from up and down to side to side.

"Hmm. And how are we going to do that? Get back to our own bodies, I mean."

Ryan stared at him. He opened his mouth to speak. And then shut it again. Because he didn't know the answer to that.

"You see, Mr Carter? When you're Mr Carter, the head teacher, you have all the answers. But when you're Mr Carter inside my body, it all gets a bit more mysterious."

Ryan took a deep breath. Then got up and walked over to the window. "Well, there must be something we can do. Apart from the imminent problem with OFFHEAD, what about the long term? We can't be in each other's bodies forever! Doesn't that worry you?"

"Forever? Yeah. But I'm enjoying it for the moment," said Mr Carter. "That's the good thing about being a kid, Mr Carter. You *live* in the moment. You don't worry about forever."

Ryan turned round to face him. "Ryan. Really. Are you honestly saying you don't feel at all uncomfortable with this whole situation?"

Mr Carter thought for a moment. Truth was, he *had* felt uncomfortable at first. Of course he had. Just being in a forty-three-year-old body – so much more full of aches and pains than his own – felt very strange, as did wearing Mr Carter's suits, and his pants, and his big shoes. Although they did fit his feet. Because his feet were Mr Carter's feet.

And this is all without even mentioning how

weird it was going for a wee. So we won't.

"Well, yes, Mr Carter, some parts of it do make me feel uncomfortable."

"I mean, what about going to the toil—"

"Yes. Let's not mention that."

"No, all right."

"But just . . . living in your house."

"You're living in my flat?"

"Of course I am! I can't live in *my* house, can I? *You're* there. And my mum would be confused and probably scared by her son's new head teacher coming round and asking to sleep there."

"How did you get in?"

Mr Carter rummaged in his suit pocket. "Doh. What's this? In your suit pocket?" He made a stupid-person face by sticking his tongue into his underlip. (Is that a word? Underlip. You know the bit of chin that is sort of also your mouth.) And said in a stupid-person voice: "*Oh. They're your keys.*"

Ryan shook his head. "Be careful, OK? I don't like the idea of you wandering around in there touching my stuff."

"I'm not touching your stuff. Apart from when I have to go to the toi—"

"I thought we weren't mentioning that?" Ryan sighed. "Anyway. I suppose I have to live with it for the moment. You being in my house."

"No. I have to live with it. It's a very boring house. There're no toys. No video games. The telly's tiny and the bed's too big."

"The bed's fine for me!"

Ryan shook his head. "Black duvet? I mean – weird. Almost creepy. And a pet wouldn't go amiss. Cheer the place up. What about a cat? Shall I get a cat?"

"I'm allergic to cats! Don't get a cat!"

"All right, calm down. Have you ever thought about getting something else apart from cheese and cold meat in the fridge?"

"Shut up! I *like* cheese and cold meat. It's better than having frozen pizza every day like your mum tells me is my absolute favourite thing, apparently."

"It's not my favourite thing."

"It isn't?"

"No. That would be *real* pizza. A bit like they make at that place opposite yours. Delivered!"

"Pardon?"

"It's very good. And not *too* expensive. Even when you've ordered all fourteen varieties on the menu."

Ryan stared at him hard. "How did you—"

Mr Carter made the stupid face again, but didn't bother to say anything this time. He just reached inside his jacket and pulled out a credit card. With the name *M. J. Carter* written clearly on it.

"*That* is illegal!" shouted Ryan.

"Well, the Devilishly Hot Chilli Explosion certainly should be. Sorry about the toilet, by the way."

"I'll call the police!"

"And tell them what?"

Ryan went very red in the face. He squeezed up his fists.

"THAT YOU'RE A VERY, VERY BAD BOY!" he shouted.

"Hm," said Mr Carter. "Well, I don't know if a Year Six boy phoning nine-nine-nine and saying his head teacher is a very, very bad boy would *actually* constitute wasting police time, but I wouldn't like to try it, personally. Anyway, point is, I don't *know* what's going to happen. I don't know when we are going to body-swap back. But I do know that right now, being you, being the head teacher of this school, I'm having – how can I put this? – a laugh. And one of the things that's *really* making it a laugh is how much everything I'm doing annoys you."

Ryan seemed about to burst with frustration. He shut his eyes and shook his head violently, as if he had a mad twitch. *"But you're destroying the school!"* he shouted. "You heard those inspectors! If you carry on like this, Bracket Wood won't just get Inadequate, it'll get an Emergency Closure notice! And then how will you feel?"

Mr Carter took this in. He frowned as if tasting the idea. Then he said: "Unbelievably . . ."

"Yes?"

". . . proud."

"What?"

"Well, as you said earlier, Mr C, I'm the naughtiest boy in the school. And I'm proud of being the naughtiest boy in the school. But how proud will I be when I get the school closed down? That will be the naughtiest thing a naughty boy has ever achieved at any school ever!"

Ryan stared at him. "Is this really who you are, Ryan Ward? A boy who thinks only about himself? What about all the other pupils at this school? Hasn't it ever occurred to you to think about what they might be feeling?"

Mr Carter laughed and shook his head. "Oh, Mr C! You're in my body. You're hanging out with my friends and my classmates. But you've still got no idea, have you, what schoolchildren of my age *want*. Do you? Because I promise you, every single pupil at this school will be *overjoyed* about the school closing down!"

For a moment, after saying this, Mr Carter felt as if he was going to laugh. Not in a friendly way – in a mad, super-villain-in-a-Marvel-or-Bond-film way. That is, it felt as if he'd given the speech that proved he was surely going to win, even if that meant things were going to turn out badly for most of the world. Even if he was, in other words, the *baddie*.

Within Mr Carter's body, therefore, something stopped Ryan laughing like this.

Hang on, he thought, *am I the baddie?*

All this was knocking about in Mr Carter's head, which was of course Ryan's head really, or at least Ryan's mind, when he was shaken out of it by a noise like a tiny sob. He looked over.

Behind the glass of the office door, he could see, standing there, Dionna Baxter. And one thing she very much *didn't* look was overjoyed.

CHAPTER 28

Kind of Forgot

"**S**o just run it past me again," said Dionna.

"I'm him," said Mr Carter, pointing at Ryan, who was looking increasingly weary. "And he's me. It's really that simple."

"*You* are Ryan."

"Yeah."

"But you look like Mr Carter."

"I know. That's the big downside."

"Ha ha," said Ryan. "Good one. Think about what

it's like for me having to live with *this* stupid face."

"Oo! That's not very teacherly of you, Mr C," said Mr Carter. "That's hurt my feelings. I may have to report you to OFFHEAD."

"OK, this is nuts," said Dionna, getting up. "I don't believe it."

"Why would we lie about it?" said Ryan. "We really stand to gain nothing from this lie."

"I have to say that me and Mr Carter are, for once, in agreement," said Mr Carter.

Dionna shook her head. It was all very strange. She had just been passing by, looking for Ryan, when she'd heard Mr Carter – who she assumed, as she might, was Mr Carter, what with him looking and sounding like Mr Carter – say that the school was going to be shut down and seeming *happy* about that. She'd glanced through the window. And then Mr Carter had beckoned to her.

She'd gone in and sat down. She'd expected to

be told off for eavesdropping or something. What she hadn't been expecting was for Mr Carter to start explaining that he wasn't Mr Carter, he was Ryan, and that Ryan was Mr Carter.

"OK. If you are Ryan—"

"No, I'm Mr Carter," said Ryan.

"Sorry," said Dionna, turning round. "If *you're* Ryan—"

"Got it," said Mr Carter.

"Why didn't you tell me this earlier?" she demanded.

"Well, I didn't think you'd believe me," said Mr Carter.

"Why do you think I believe you now?"

Mr Carter shrugged. "I dunno. You've seen all the new rules I've made. They're not very old-style Mr Carter-ish, are they? They're more old-style Ryan-ish, aren't they?"

Ryan nodded in agreement. "Yes. I don't approve

of any of them," he said.

"And also –" said Mr Carter, pointing to Ryan – "*he's* here now, agreeing with me. Why would Ryan do that?"

Dionna thought for a moment. "It could be one of his pranks."

"One of his pranks," said Ryan wearily, "that he'd got the most anti-prankster head teacher of all time to come in on?"

Now, Mr Carter nodded in agreement.

Dionna shook her head and sat down again, looking at him closely. "I can't believe it, Ryan. *You're* in Mr Carter's body? Isn't that weird? What about going to the toi—"

"We've agreed not to discuss that," said Ryan.

"It's best," said Mr Carter.

Dionna looked from one to the other. "Are you living in his house?" she said to Ryan. (That is, Mr Carter.)

"Yep."

"Ordered pizzas on his credit card yet?"

"Fourteen. In one night."

"Hmm," she said. "Maybe it *is* you. But . . . OK. What's my mum's name?"

"Esther."

"Who's my favourite singer?"

"Beyoncé."

"Who's my best friend?"

Mr Carter paused. Ryan looked at him, raising an eyebrow.

"Well . . . me. I hope. I mean him," said Mr Carter, pointing at Ryan.

Dionna nodded. She seemed to be taking her time about what to say next.

And then she said, "But I just heard you say that the school was going to close down. Because of what you've done. And that you were proud of that, pleased about it!"

"Well," said Mr Carter. "Um . . . yeah."

"Even though you *know* that would be really, really upsetting for me because I'd have to go back to Oakcroft!"

"Oh," said Mr Carter.

He felt a falling in his stomach. He knew this was bad and was about to say, "Thing is, what with all the changing-bodies thing, and the being-head-teacher thing, and the doing-whatever-I-like-with-the-school thing . . . I kind of forgot about that." But he didn't. Mainly because he realised it wouldn't help much.

"And so you know what?" she said, getting up. "I'm not sure you *are* Ryan. Or at least, I'm not sure you are my best friend." She was at the door by now, looking back into the room. "Because my best friend would never, ever do that to me!"

There was a chance at this point, perhaps, for Mr Carter to say, "OK, no, you're right, I'll do something to stop that happening."

But he didn't say this either. Because he could see Ryan smirking at him and he didn't want to back down from his former triumph about the school closing. So he just looked at her and shrugged.

Like a naughty, told-off little boy.

Which meant that Dionna shook her head, raised her eyebrows and went out, slamming the door.

"Oh dear," said Ryan, still smirking.

CHAPTER 29

Other

"Sorry, Head Teacher," said Tina Ward, who was waiting outside the school gates to pick up her son. She had Holly with her in a pushchair.

Mr Carter wasn't really listening. He was looking around. He was looking, in fact, for Dionna, who had run away just after he'd seen her in the office. He wanted to reassure her that everything would be OK. Although he hadn't quite worked out how to do that yet. Or indeed whether it would be.

"What?" said Mr Carter distractedly.

"Oh, never mind," said Tina crossly. She had thought about turning over a new leaf with him, by apologising for Ryan's behaviour, but now that he'd just ignored her she was convinced that he was not a nice person all over again.

"About what?" said Ryan, appearing at the gates. "What are you talking to him for?"

"No, Yan!" said Holly. Then, looking questioningly at Mr Carter, she added, "Yan?"

"I heard!" said Tina, turning to her son. "I heard you had to go to his office again! I had hoped the new head might have led to a change in you!"

"I see," said Ryan, nodding. "Well, in a sense, it has . . . I'm quite the reformed character."

Tina frowned. Ryan was still clearly playing up, speaking in this posh, grown-up way that he'd been doing for a while now. It was annoying.

"Anyway! Nice to see you, Mum!" said Mr Carter,

turning to face her properly. Dionna was nowhere to be seen, so – in a rather typical eleven-year-old-boy way – he just decided not to worry any more about the thing that had been really worrying him.

"I beg your pardon?" said Tina.

And also he'd said *Mum*. So that was something else to worry about.

"I said . . . I said . . ."

"Yes . . . Mr Carter!" said Ryan fiercely. "*What* did you say?"

"I said . . . I said, 'That's all right, chum!'"

Tina frowned. "I beg your pardon? Again?"

"It's a new policy! I consider teacher-parent friendliness very important! So all staff will now make sure they address all parents as 'mate', 'pal', 'me old mucker' or indeed . . . 'chum'!" said Mr Carter hurriedly.

Ryan stared at him. Then very slowly shook his head.

"OK," said Tina. She frowned, but laughed. And added, "Mate!"

"Thanks, buddy!" said Mr Carter. This made her laugh more.

"That's all right, comrade!" said Tina through her laughter.

"Friend!" said Mr Carter in a squeaky high voice, putting both his thumbs up. "Ooh, friend!"

This made Tina bellow with laughter.

"Hey! Ryan! Mr Carter knows that meme!" she said. "You know, the one that you showed me – from that TV show—"

Luckily for Ryan – who was looking very confused and still shaking his head – this was the moment Holly decided to shout again, pointing at him.

"'No Yan! *No Yan!*"

"Oh, not again!" said Tina. "It *is* Ryan, Holly!"

"No Yan! Other! Other!"

"Yes," said Ryan. "Exactly. The thing is, Ti— Mum,

I genuinely believe that the baby might possess some kind of insight here. Did you hear her call me 'other'? As in, not Ryan."

"Oh, for goodness' sake," said Tina. "You know perfectly well she's saying 'brother'. You know she never says words properly."

"Doesn't she?" said Ryan. "Hm. It's never too early to try phonics, I always say."

Tina just stared at him.

"Yes, well, anyway, my point is I think she may be actually perceiving the truth in a deeper way than you as an adult can comprehend, and—"

"Ryan! Stop talking like that. And go and get in the car!"

"Car? You – I mean, we only live over there!"

"Yes, but we're not going home. We're going to see Annie."

"'Ocolate!" said Holly, trying a different tack.

Tina tutted. "Excuse me a moment," she said,

pushing the chair away a little and crouching down to sort out the baby.

"Who's Annie?" Ryan asked Mr Carter quietly.

"My great-aunt. Mum's aunt," replied Mr Carter.

"Oh super. What's she like?"

"Nice. But farts a lot. I mean, like, *a lot*."

Ryan sighed. "Great. Really. Great."

"It is kind of funny."

"Now, you see, Ryan, that is typical of you. I'm sure it's not her fault if she has stomach issues. And it's very important to take that kind of issue in old people seriously."

"OK. I've always found the only way to get through it is to laugh about it. She doesn't seem to mind. But whatevs."

Tina came back to them, pushing the pushchair.

"I thought I told you to get in the car!" she said to Ryan. "I'm sorry, Mr Carter, I really don't know what's got into him at the moment."

"I really don't know either, pardner!" said Mr Carter.

"Friend!" said Tina in a squeaky voice, doing the thumbs-up thing.

Then Mr Carter joined in and together they went, "Ooh, friend! Friend! Teacher friend! Parent friend!"

And it seemed as if they were never going to stop. So Ryan sighed and walked towards the car.

CHAPTER 30

BRRASSSSSHHHHHHHHHHHHHHOOOOOC

"**O**MG," said Tina, "I'm not even joking. But *something* has happened to that man. Something good."

"Has it," said Ryan flatly. They were sitting together on a sofa in Aunt Annie's living room. Aunt Annie herself, a tiny woman with an enormous behind, had gone to make some tea. The living room looked as if it had last been decorated in 1957. There were a lot of glass cabinets dotted around the place, containing plates and mugs commemorating various events in the life of the British royal family. A very old, very thin-looking cat with no teeth stared at them from the opposite sofa.

"Yes! Just now, I found myself really warming to him. But before . . . I mean there was that whole business with your funny fainting spell and the hospital, which turned me right against him. And then he seemed so stuffy and strict at the Parents' Open Afternoon. And of course he was so angry with you about the tortoise thing, which was, let's face it, quite funny."

"Was it."

"Yes. Up with your best."

"Hm."

"So . . . I didn't take to him at all."

"Didn't you," said Ryan.

"No, he seemed a right—"

"Yes, all right, Tina," said Ryan. "Can you stop

going on about it? You haven't stopped talking about him all the way here."

Tina shrugged. "Oh well. All I'm saying is he seems to have loosened up a lot. Which by the way is the opposite of what seems to have happened to you. And I've told you – stop calling me Tina!"

"Hello, loves!" said Aunt Annie, coming in with a china teapot and some cups on a tray that had a picture of a steam train on it. "Shall I be mother?"

She set the tray down in front of Tina and Ryan.

"'Ake! 'Ake! 'Ake!"

"She hasn't made any cake, darling," said Tina to Holly, who was on her knee, grabbing at the air.

"'Iscuit?"

"Sorry, Annie, have you got any?" asked Tina.

"Benny?" said Annie, looking round as she poured the tea. "He's dead. This cat's called Chairman Meow."

"No, Annie," said Tina more loudly. "Switch

your hearing aid on!"

"John? He died years ago!"

"Your hearing aid!" She pointed at her aunt's ear, where indeed there was a hearing aid lodged inside. "It's off!"

"Yes, he had a very bad cough," she said, handing over a cup to Tina. She settled herself down on the armchair. "That's what killed him." *BRRRRRAAAPPP!*

There was a pause after this for about a split second, before Holly burst out laughing.

"Ha ha ha ha ha! 'Art! 'Art!"

"What are you saying? What are you saying, little one?" said Annie in an old-lady-speaking-to-a-baby voice, bending her face down close to Holly's and wrinkling her nose. And to be honest, so were Tina and Ryan – and now, indeed the baby – but for different reasons.

"She's so adorable, isn't she? The sweetest thing."
FRRALLLLPPPPBsssssssshhhh . . .

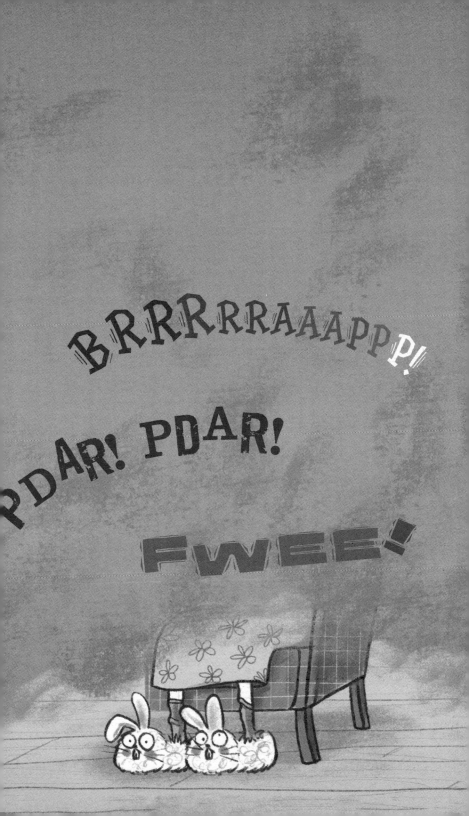

"Oh dear," said Tina, "she's always worse when she forgets to put the hearing aid on. It's like she can't hear that she's doing it."

"Can't she . . ." said Ryan, *"feel* that she's—".

"I don't think she's got much feeling . . . you know . . . *around there.*"

Tina said the words *around there* in a whisper, which Ryan felt was frankly unnecessary.

"Have a cup of tea, Ryan. Three sugars?" *BLAP!*

"Er, no, thank you. I take it black, no sugar."

"Could you hear something then?" said Aunt Annie as she dropped three sugar lumps into Ryan's milky tea and handed it over. "Like a distant quack. Like someone stood on a duck's foot?"

"Um . . ."

PDAR! PDAR!

"'Art! 'Art!"

"What *are* you saying, little one?"

"'Iscuit?"

"Should we do something?" said Ryan to Tina under his breath while Aunt Annie's attention was distracted. Aunt Annie had at this point got up from the sofa and was bending over to put her face close to the baby's. That's right. Bending over.

"What do you mean?" said Tina.

"Well . . . call a doctor. I mean, something's clearly wrong. The responsible thing to do would be to get some medical help."

Tina frowned at him. "She's been like this for years! There's nothing wrong with her. And, y'know, better out than in. It would just upset her to point it out. Anyway, you normally just laugh at it!"

"Well, that's awful. I shouldn't have done. I'm a – a changed man!"

"Oh yes, I forgot," said Tina. "You're actually your new head teacher!"

"Yes! I am! Isn't this proof that it's true? Because I'm not laughing?"

Tina looked at him.

"Crip!"

"Dip? You want a dip? That's very grown-up. Houmous?" *BLAP!* "Yoghurt?" *FNNNARRRR!* "Taramasalata?" *RRITTBAH!*

"We'll see," said Tina.

Ryan frowned. Did Tina Ward really think that just because – *FDAP! NISH!* – he, who was really not an eleven-year-old boy – *TIFTER!* – but a responsible, sensible, serious forty-three-year-old head teacher – *DING!* – would collapse into laughter just because Aunt Annie had – *JAHWOBBLE!* – a small – *PATOOSH!* – well, not so small – *FWEE!* – problem with her digestion?

"What about the smell?" said Ryan.

"It's getting worse, I agree," said Tina.

"No. I mean about her not knowing she's doing it. Surely even if Aunt Annie is deaf and a little . . . numb . . . downstairs . . . her nose works, doesn't it?"

Which, to be fair, was a relevant question to ask at this point, as the air in the room – never that fresh, frankly – was turning a little green.

"'Oo! 'Oo! 'Ells of 'oo!"

"What does Holly want? Blue? I've got a crayon somewhere— Oh my goodness." Aunt Annie sat back down on her chair. "*What* is that smell? Dearie, dearie me. Have you noticed it, Tina? Ryan? Oh, I say, that's *awful*."

Ryan turned to Tina with an I *told you so* expression. He folded his arms as if to say, Now, *please, can we take this seriously*?

"You know what this means?" continued Annie, turning to her side. "Chairman! Chairman Meow!"

The ancient cat – quite surprisingly, since one might have assumed him to be deafer even than his owner – looked up, confused.

"Please stop doing that, you smelly cat! I've told you before. You have to try to control your flatulence!" *BRRRRING!* "It's making a terrible smell!" *NOOOSH!* "And it's antisocial for everyone here!" *FDAP! FFFLING! STREEEEEESH!* "Do you understand?"

"Meow."

"Good."

BRRASHHHHHHHHHHHHHHOOOOOO.

She lifted up the teapot, smiling. "Anyone for more tea?"

And at that point Ryan burst out laughing. He laughed and laughed and laughed in a way that the head teacher inside him for many years had not. He laughed so much, in fact, that he farted.

CHAPTER 31
A Message For Mr Carter

While Ryan was at Aunt Annie's, Mr Carter went back to Mr Carter's flat. He was still troubled about Dionna. He took off the suit jacket and sat on Mr Carter's not very comfy black leather sofa, wondering what to do. He tried watching TV, but not only was the screen quite tiny – all the series links were for channels called things like "History" and "Geographic" and "Natural", so there wasn't anything exciting recorded for him to watch.

Perhaps I should call Mum, he thought. *She would know what's best.*

Then he realised he couldn't do that. Or, at least, it would take a lot of explaining and she wouldn't believe him. And even if she did he doubted that at the end of it she'd be very interested in answering the question, "So, anyway, what should I say to Dionna to make her like me again?"

He got up and rummaged through the fourteen cardboard pizza boxes strewn around the living room to see if there were any bits of delicious stuffed crust left. But since he'd already done this last night, there weren't. He went back to the jacket, took out Mr Carter's credit card and went over to the phone.

When he picked up the receiver, though, he wasn't sure about ordering pizza again – he didn't know how much money Mr Carter actually had in his bank account and he didn't want to spend it *all* on pizza.

Plus it didn't feel quite as thrilling and fun just to do it again. He suddenly had an image of him ordering pizza every night, stretching into the future, and it didn't feel fun at all.

In truth, he wasn't that hungry. He just felt a tiny bit lonely. He even thought to himself, looking at the boxes, 'Izza. Just because it was what his baby sister would have said. Or maybe 'izza 'ox. He'd like to have heard that. It would've made him laugh and cheered him up.

Then he noticed that on the main phone console there was a light blinking. Which meant there was a message for him. Well, not for him. For Mr Carter. So maybe he should ignore it.

But, then again, it was blinking. And Ryan felt a tiny bit lonely. At least it would be good hearing another voice. So he pressed the button.

"Hello . . ." said a worried-sounding female voice on the machine. "This is a message for Mr Carter.

It's Zadie at St Winifred's. Your mum has taken a bit of a turn for the worse, I'm afraid. She's stable at the moment, but maybe you should come down as soon as you can. Thanks, all the best. Zadie. Oh, I said that already. Anyway, bye."

CHAPTER 32

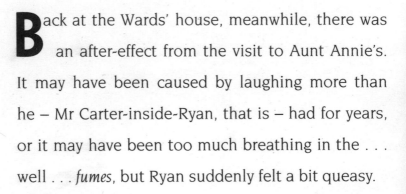

Really Nice

Back at the Wards' house, meanwhile, there was an after-effect from the visit to Aunt Annie's. It may have been caused by laughing more than he – Mr Carter-inside-Ryan, that is – had for years, or it may have been too much breathing in the . . . well . . . *fumes*, but Ryan suddenly felt a bit queasy.

So he went to bed. Mr Carter had been ill quite a lot when he was a child, but it still felt strange, as a grown man, to go to bed at 6pm, particularly under a duvet with pirates on it (a duvet, in fact, that Ryan-in-Ryan's-body had been telling Tina for some time that *he'd* grown out of).

But then Tina came in and asked him if he was OK. And Ryan said he still felt a bit sick, but not too bad. So she put a hand on his forehead and kissed him on the cheek, and then tucked him in and told him not to worry – she was sure he'd feel better soon.

And that *didn't* feel strange. That felt nice. Really nice.

CHAPTER 33
That's My Problem

S tanding outside Mrs Carter's room, waiting to be let inside by the nurse, Mr Carter, feeling very much like who he really was – Ryan – wondered why he'd come.

In Mr Carter's flat, having heard the message, he'd suddenly felt he should. In the forefront of his mind, it was just that he felt sorry for Mr Carter's mum – he didn't think that she should have to be on her own in hospital just because he and her son had switched bodies. (He realised after thinking this that the word "just" was a bit odd in this sentence.)

But in the back of his mind he knew it was because he'd wanted to talk to his mum – and Mrs Carter, at this moment, kind of *was* his mum.

It was a funny sort of hospital, St Winifred's. Mr Carter had got there easily – he'd passed it many times (as Ryan) on the way to and from school – but he'd never been inside before. It didn't have a big reception area, like most hospitals, with lots of people queuing and babies crying and the odd man with a bleeding head shouting at his wife about how he hadn't been drinking, well not that much, anyway. It was very quiet and carpeted and calm, more like the bed and breakfast in Dorset to which his mum took him and Holly for their summer holidays. And instead of having to spend ages with a harassed-looking person in front of a computer trying to work out which ward the patient he was trying to visit was in, Zadie the nurse just met him at the door and led him across the hallway to Mrs Carter's room.

"I don't know if she's awake," said Zadie in a very hushed voice. "She's been sleeping a lot."

"OK," said Mr Carter.

"But I'm sure she'll be pleased to see you. If she wakes up."

Mr Carter nodded. But, inside, Ryan was nervous. Mrs Carter sounded sicker than he'd realised. Plus, the idea of anyone being pleased to see Mr Carter seemed weird to him. In fact, the idea of Mr Carter having a mum – of *any* teacher having a mum or dad – had never really occurred to him before. But there it was, a sign on the outside of the door: GRACE CARTER.

Quietly, Zadie opened the door. Inside was a pleasant room, all painted in white, with a view of a garden through the window. At the far end of the room stood a bed. In it, propped up a little by pillows, was an old lady, asleep. She had white hair and a sweet face. You wouldn't have known she was ill, except for a tube that went from a machine at the side of the bed into her nose.

"I'll leave you. Just call if you need anything," said Zadie, shutting the door.

Don't, Mr Carter wanted to say. *Don't leave.* But he was stuck being an adult – being more of an adult than he'd had to be so far – and so he just nodded.

He went over to the bed. Grace Carter was breathing in a shallow way. As he sat down on the chair next to the bed, her eyes half opened. She smiled and frowned at the same time, as if the smiling caused her some pain.

"Michael . . ." she said. "How nice of you to come."

Michael? thought Mr Carter. *Who's Michael?*

Then he realised. *Oh. It's me. Well, Mr Carter.*

"Er . . . that's OK," he said uncertainly. Then more uncertainly, "How are you?"

She smiled again, and frowned again. "You know.

237

I've been better. But mustn't complain."

"Well. You could."

She opened her eyes a bit more. "Pardon?"

"I'm just saying. If I were you, I'd be complaining a lot. I always complain when I'm ill. My—" He was about to say "mum says" and then remembered that would sound strange.

Grace shook her head, but continued to smile. "Not really, Michael. You were always very stoic."

"Stow-ick?"

"Yes. When you were ill, which was quite a lot when you were little, you would always just sit there and hardly ask for anything. It was all I could do to get you to stay off school."

"Oh. Right. Yeah. I forgot."

Grace carried on looking at him. Then she said, "You know, darling . . . now that we're talking about all that, about things in the past, I don't want to leave too many things unsaid."

"Right," he said, not really understanding what this meant.

"I think that happens a lot. You know. At times like these. When there maybe isn't much time left . . . and then people – they regret it. They regret what they didn't say."

"Right."

"And I think Dad, when he was alive, maybe encouraged you to be a little . . . you know . . . stiff upper lip and all that. To not really say how you feel because he wasn't very comfy, was he, with feelings? And I wouldn't want you to be like that. To think you couldn't say how you feel."

"OK."

"Because even though you are like your father in many ways, in some other ways – like when I look at you now – I see the little boy inside you. The little boy you once were. He's still there, I think, even though he's forced to wear this big stern grown-up suit-of-armour of a body the whole time."

She reached out and he took her hand in his. It was thin and light, but warm. She was looking at him more closely now. "Michael. Are you crying?"

"Am I?" He realised he was.

"Oh dear. I'm sorry. You *never* cry."

He wiped his eyes with the back of his hand, the one that wasn't holding hers, and sniffed. "Sorry."

"No, it's OK, Michael. Really. That's exactly what I'm talking about." She paused, still smiling, but a tear, just one, dropped slowly from her right eye, shining down her cheek. "I'm glad. Really."

She squeezed his hand.

"Hello," said Zadie, coming softly into the room. "Sorry, Grace – Michael – but it's time for Grace to have some of her pain-killing medication."

Mr Carter looked round. Grace let go of his hand. She nodded.

"You'd better go, darling. Thank you so much for coming. I know you have a lot of work to do."

He nodded, and got up. Zadie went round the other side of Grace and started preparing a syringe.

"Especially with the new school. How's it going?"

"Um . . ." said Mr Carter, putting his coat back on. "Well, actually, it might get closed down. If we fail the inspection which is in . . . six days' time." Suddenly, and with a sharp pang, he thought of Dionna.

"You think you can turn it round?" she asked.

"Um . . ." he said again. This was a tough one. But all at once it came to him – to Ryan Ward, inside the body of Michael Carter, the head teacher of Bracket Wood School; he knew *exactly* what to say. "Listen. Mum. Don't you worry about that. That's *my* problem."

And he walked out of the door.

PART FOUR
HEAD
TO
HEAD
BRACKET WOOD
VS
OAKCROFT

CHAPTER 34

A Hubbub

"**O**K, Bracket Wood! Quiet down! Come on!" Mr Barrington was saying. Mr Carter had called an emergency assembly. "Good morning, Bracket Wood!"

"Good morning, Mr Bummington!" said most of the school. Unfortunately for Mr Bummington – sorry, Barrington – the spirit of Mr Carter, or rather of Ryan-as-Mr Carter, had taken root at Bracket Wood. Those who were not shouting this rude version of his name back at him were making faces, laughing, blowing raspberries, eating sweets, jumping up and down or simply not listening.

"Oh dear. Dear, dear, dear," said Mr Barrington.

"Shush!" cried Mrs Wang.

"Stop it!" cried Miss Finch.

"Oh, my head!" cried Miss Gerard.

"What are we going to do?" said Mr Barrington to the other teachers in desperation over the noise. "OFFHEAD are coming back! We're all going to lose our jobs!"

"Where's the head?" asked Mrs Wang.

"I don't know! He's vanished! He's turned the school into this! And then just disappear—"

PHWEEEEEEEEEEEE!

The very loud, very high sound pierced the noise in the assembly hall. Everyone looked round to see Mr Carter standing at the door, whistle in hand.

"Right!" he said. "We have work to do!"

"We do?" said Mr Barrington.

"That's right, Mr Barrington," he said, striding on to the stage. "Good morning, Bracket Wood!"

"Good morning, Mr Carter!" said the school. Except for one person.

"Who said *Farter*?"

Barry Bennett put his hand up.

"OK, Barry. Very funny. It does rhyme with my name. But don't do it again. It's not respectful."

"But I though—"

"I don't care what you thought. Don't do it again."

Barry, a bit abashed, put his hand down.

"So. Look. Guys. We have a problem. As some of you may remember, two grown-ups turned up yesterday out of nowhere at lunchtime. Turns out they were OFFHEAD. Yeah!"

"What's OFFHEAD?" said Scarlet.

"Is it like Apple? Or Microsoft?" asked Stirling.

"They're inspectors. Government inspectors. And

basically they can shut the school down."

"HOORAY!" shouted Morris Fawcett, grinning.

"No, not hooray. And it should be clear to all of you that it's *not*-hooray by the fact that *Morris* decided to shout that."

Morris stopped grinning.

"Look, I know it might sound great, the school being shut down. But at the end of the day, we – I mean you – do all have to go to school *somewhere*. And if it wasn't here it would probably be somewhere worse. And, y'know, it's not *that* bad here."

"What about the toilets?"

"Yes, all right, Ellie, the toilets are terrible. And some of the teachers, of course, but apart from that—"

Mr Barrington, Miss Gerard, Miss Finch and Mrs Wang all looked at each other deadpan.

"—it's all right. I mean this is where we get to spend time with our friends. Our . . ."

And here Mr Carter searched out a face. Yes. There she was, sitting at the back of the room. Dionna.

". . . *best* friends."

There was a hubbub following this, and a murmur. Voices could be heard saying, "He's got a point," and, "I don't know if I'd like to go anywhere else," and, "We could clean the toilets ourselves," and in Morris Fawcett's case, "Should I have said 'hip-hip'?" But Mr Carter didn't pay any attention to that. He kept on looking at Dionna. Whose face, eventually, broke into a smile.

CHAPTER 35

All Very Well

"**O**K!" Mr Carter said to the gathered pupils. "So. What are we gonna do? We've got a week. Just under."

"Well," said Mr Barrington, "we could . . . I mean if you don't mind, Headmaster . . . you know . . . drop some of those rules you made on your first day. The ones about running in the corridor and turning round in class."

"Yes. OK."

A groan went up from the hall.

"But I haven't even got my praise points for that yet!" shouted Isla Fawcett. "And I turned round three hundred times in English alone!"

"Does this mean I needn't have come to school in this?" said Alfie Moore.

Everyone looked over. Alfie was wearing a top hat with a picture of Mr Barrington on it, except instead of his face under the hat there was a cartoon of a monkey's very pink bum.

"Sorry . . . but yes. Breaks my heart," said Mr Carter.

Sadly Alfie took it off.

"And," said L'Shaniqua, who had wandered in from the dining hall, "we're going back to normal food? Because we've made a strawberry-jelly pie with chips for lunch."

"Potato chips?"

"No, chocolate. But in the shape of chips."

"HOOR—"

"No, Morris. Sorry. Yes. Normal food again. Oliver-approved."

Another groan.

"Although maybe keep the chocolate chips for dessert."

The groan stopped.

"This is all very well," said a voice, "but it's not going to be enough."

It was Ryan. He'd got up from his cross-legged position and was now standing near the front of the assembly-hall stage.

"None of that is going to save the school," he said.

CHAPTER 36
Bring It On

"**H**ow do you mean?" said Mr Carter.

"Well . . ." said Ryan, getting on the stage and going towards the lectern. "This school was already under threat. OFFHEAD have been unhappy with it for a while. Getting it back to how it was before isn't going to get it any more than another Inadequate. Which will still mean closure."

"It will?"

"It will."

Mr Carter frowned. His shoulders slumped.

"So what shall we do?"

If any of the pupils or teachers at Bracket Wood thought it was a little odd at this point for the head teacher to be asking the naughtiest boy in the school what they should do, they didn't show it. Possibly because things had been a little weird at the school for a while now.

"I think," said Ryan, "that what's needed is an idea. An event. Something that could be put on here for the benefit of the OFFHEAD inspectors that makes the school seem BETTER than it normally is."

"Like what?"

Ryan laughed somewhat scornfully. It didn't sound like his normal laugh. "Well, *Mr Carter.* I think that very much needs to come from *you.* Seeing as you're the head teacher. Aren't you?"

Mr Carter looked at him. He took a deep breath.

"Yes. Yes. I am. And so I *have* an idea."

"Oh," said Ryan, nodding. "Great. Looking forward to hearing this. What is it?"

"It's . . ."

"Yes?"

"It's . . ."

"Yes?" Ryan stuck his hands behind his ears, pushing them forward. "Really. I'm all ears."

"It's . . ." Mr Carter looked out towards the full assembly hall. "To throw it open to the floor. To the school. To the kids! And then choose the best idea!"

"Right," said Ryan. "Great. That's gonna work."

"Anyone?"

"We build a swimming pool in the playground and fill it with custard! And then have custard swimming races."

"OK, thanks, Caspar. Maybe something *easier* than that?"

"Calling Barrington Bummington! Except we all do it at once!"

"Yes, you see, Morris, we've stopped doing that. We've stopped . . . just doing naughty stuff."

"Have we? When?"

"It's going well, Mr Carter, isn't it?" said Ryan.

"Debate!" shouted a girl's voice.

Dionna's voice.

"Sorry?" said Ryan.

"We kind of are," said Mr Carter. "In a way. Aren't we." He pointed at Ryan. "Me and him. Debating."

"No, you're not," she said. "That's not debating. In a proper debate there are two teams, with, like, two people on them. They're called Houses. And you have a motion, something serious and clever, like 'This House Believes that the Best Things in

Life are Free' or 'This House Believes that Freedom of Speech is the Basis of a Just Society'. That's called the motion. And then one House argues for the motion and one against it. And then some judges decide who wins. Which could be the OFFHEAD inspectors."

A murmur went round the assembly hall in response to this.

Mr Carter looked at Ryan. He raised an eyebrow.

Ryan put his hand on his chin, stroking it. Not for the first time since he'd been transformed into her best friend, the head teacher inside Ryan thought, *That Dionna Baxter is really quite impressive.*

"You know what?" he said. "That isn't a terrible idea."

"It's a brilliant idea! Well done, Dionna!" Mr Carter grinned.

"But," continued Ryan, "if we really want to stage something that will impress the OFFHEAD inspectors, I don't think a debate just between two teams made up of Bracket Wood pupils is going to do it. I think we need to show them this school can compete with other schools. I think we need to put on a debate where Bracket Wood takes on, and beats, another school – one that's been ranked GOOD or even OUTSTANDING."

"Yes!" said Mr Carter.

"Yes!" said Mr Barrington, getting caught up in it all.

"YEEESSS!" said the children in the hall.

"Yaay . . ." said Miss Gerard with a yawn, slumping against the back wall.

"So! Which school are you thinking of?" said Mr Carter.

"I'm thinking, Head Teacher, of the only school in the area with a ranking of OUTSTANDING. Oakcroft."

Everyone immediately went quiet. They all glanced at each other. The teachers frowned.

Mr Carter gulped and said, "Oakcroft?"

Ryan nodded.

"The really posh school that has loads of money and brilliant results and whose debating team I believe also won the National Debating Challenge three years running?" asked Mr Carter.

Ryan nodded again.

"But . . . what if we lose? Which, you know . . . is really possible? Won't that make it worse? In front of the inspectors?"

Ryan nodded for the third time.

"I think that may just be the risk we have to take," he said.

Mr Carter turned and looked with some fear towards Dionna, who was still standing at the back of the hall, her face a blank mask.

But then, gradually, that blank mask turned into a face that was fierce, that was confident, that was defiant.

"Bring. It. On!" she shouted.

CHAPTER 37
Minor-royal-face

It was all hands on deck at Bracket Wood that week. All the mad rules that Mr Carter had made since coming back from hospital were reversed. A new healthy lunch menu that actually did get approved by Jamie Oliver – Scarlet and Stirling sent it to him on Instagram – was brought in to replace the crazy sweet stuff (which meant that they had loads of cake mix left over). The tortoises were spruced up and any human underwear removed from them. Even the toilets were finally cleaned and a plumber brought in to unblock the three that had been blocked since 1999.

It was amazing that they managed to get all this done so quickly. But a new spirit of cooperation seemed to have entered Bracket Wood, with staff and pupils working happily together. Ryan, with Mr Carter, headed up a school council made up of the most enterprising, hardworking children there, and they helped to make sure that all the ideas of the smart new regime were actually enacted.

Amazingly, Ryan and Mr Carter were actually getting on. It was as if they both realised something. Which was that neither of them knew when – or even if – they would get back to their own bodies, but in the meantime it wouldn't help either of them for the school to be shut down. So they might as well work together.

And since they were working together Ryan had

come along on the day when Mr Carter and Dionna had gone to meet Oakcroft's head teacher.

"COME!" said Mrs Valentine-Fine OBE.

Mr Carter looked a bit confused. They were standing outside her wood-panelled door at the end of a long wood-panelled corridor. Although there were children milling about nearby, it was terrifically silent. There was no shouting or screaming, no bumps or bangs from anyone being tripped over, or drinks spilling, or lockers being slammed. It sounded, in other words, very different from anywhere at Bracket Wood.

"She means in," said Ryan.

"Yeah, posh people sometimes just say 'Come!' when they mean come in," said Dionna.

"COME!"

"I think we'd better go in," said Ryan.

Inside, it was even quieter than outside. The room was covered with a very plush carpet. The wood panelling was even more woody and polished than outside. It felt like the sort of room where there should be no sound except for the ticking of a grandfather clock. But since there wasn't one of those there was no sound at all. Until it was broken by . . .

"AH! IT'S THE BRACKET WOOD GANG! HOORAH!"

"Oh blimey!" said Mr Carter, on realising it was Mrs Valentine-Fine OBE speaking from behind her desk. Well, a bit more than speaking.

"I BEG YOUR PARDON?"

"Well, I thought you were just speaking like that because we were on the other side of the door. But it turns out you speak like that all the time!"

"SPEAK LIKE WHAT ALL THE TIME?"

Mrs Valentine-Fine OBE was a frightening-looking woman. For a start, her hair, which she wore in a kind of standing-up wavy block, was bright orange, similar in tone to Donald Trump's skin. Although not physically that large, she seemed to take up an enormous amount of space in the room. She wore a bright red dress that clashed very badly with her hair. And on her bosom – can I say bosom? Oh well, I have – rested a pair of glasses on a chain.

She also didn't seem to know when she was shouting.

MRS VALENTINE - FINE
OBE

"Mrs Valentine-Fine—" said Ryan smoothly.

"OBE!" said Mrs Valentine-Fine. OBE.

"I beg your pardon?"

"Mrs Valentine-Fine, as I'm sure most well-informed people know," said a voice off to one side, "has an honour bestowed personally by Her Majesty the Queen, blessed be she, for services to education."

Ryan and Mr Carter looked over. Standing to one side were a girl and a boy. They were presumably Year Sixes, but looked much older. The girl was tall with a sharp, beaky nose and short hair worn in a stern side parting. She was standing with her arms folded, staring directly at them. The boy, even taller, had long blond hair and was standing with one arm up against the wall of the head teacher's room, as if he was a model. "Yuh. She got it for, like, being amazeballs at teaching stuff. I mean, my great-aunt really told her she was, like, the best."

"Your great-aunt?" said Mr Carter.

"Oh, soz. My great-aunt is, like, Her Maj. Like, Liz Two. Like, Send Her Victorious, Happy and whatevs."

"And," said the girl, as Mr Carter and Ryan stared open-mouthed, "Mrs Valentine-Fine OBE therefore prefers to be addressed as Mrs Valentine-Fine OBE."

"I DO! THAT IS CORRECT. THANK YOU, BELINDA. THANK YOU, TOBY!" said Mrs Valentine-Fine OBE, picking up her glasses off her bosom – oh no, I've said it again! – and putting them on her nose as if to peer more carefully at these strange visitors. "NOW. WHAT CAN WE DO FOR YOU?"

"Well," said Ryan, "I think our head can explain. Can't you, Mr Carter?"

"That bloke is the queen's nephew?" said Mr Carter.

"Great-nephew. Apparently. Anyway, can't you, Mr Carter?"

"What?"

"Oh, heavens. Explain. What we are doing here."

"Oh. Yeah." Mr Carter turned to Mrs Valentine-Fine OBE. "We'd like to challenge you to a debate!"

"SORRY?"

"You. V us. A debate. At our place, Monday next week. Judged by OFFHEAD. What do you say?"

Mrs Valentine-Fine OBE frowned. She looked over at Belinda and Toby, who frowned as well. Then she said, "WELL, I THINK WHAT WE WOULD SAY IS . . ."

And together they all went . . .

"HA! HA! HA! HA! HA! HA!"

They all finished at the same time, which was quite impressive. Mr Carter and Ryan looked at each other.

"What, just that?" said Mr Carter. "Laughing?"

"AH HA! HA! HA! HA! HA! HA!"

Although this time they didn't finish on quite the

same beat. "HA! HA . . . like, HA!" went Toby.

"I'M SO SORRY, MR CARTER. I DON'T MEAN TO LAUGH, BUT THIS SCHOOL HAS WON THE NATIONAL SCHOOLS' DEBATING CHAMPIONSHIP FIFTEEN YEARS RUNNING! AND BRACKET WOOD IS . . . WELL . . . BRACKET WOOD. YOU KNOW?"

Mr Carter looked at her. Inside, the boy who'd gone to Bracket Wood for the last six years, and who had spent most of that time pranking teachers and making fun of it, felt strangely angry.

"No," he said. "I *don't* know what you mean!"

"And neither," said Ryan, standing side by side with him, "do I!"

Mrs Valentine-Fine OBE took off her glasses and replaced them on her you-know-where. She raised an eyebrow, unused to being challenged in any way. She stood up as if she was going to tell them both off. But before she could open her mouth to speak, Belinda said, "What about you, Dionna?"

Everyone looked round. At that point, Mr Carter realised that Dionna had not said a word since they'd come in to the office. She was deliberately looking down, not at Belinda. Who continued, with a sly smile on her face.

"Dionna? It is you, isn't it? Dionna Baxter? Who used to go here?"

"Oh, what, Bels?" said Toby. "The scholarship girl? Is that her? The one with the mum from Nigeria? But not like a princess or anything, just literally from Nigeria? Kra-Kra!"

"DIONNA! HOW WONDERFUL! AND YOU OF COURSE WERE ACTUALLY A JUNIOR MEMBER OF OUR DEBATING TEAM. BEFORE YOU SADLY . . . . HAD TO LEAVE!"

"Yes, that was very sad," said Belinda, but she didn't look at all sad. "Are you happier now, Dionna? At . . . what's it called again, Tobes?"

"Placket Hood?"

"Yes. Are you happier at Placket Hood?"

Mr Carter and Ryan exchanged glances. But Dionna looked up slowly and met Belinda's eye. And said calmly, "I am, Belinda, thank you. Perfectly happy. Although . . ."

"Yes?" said Belinda, looking as if she was eager to hear this.

". . . not as happy as I will be when me and the rest of the BRACKET WOOD debating team take you and minor-royal-face here down! See you next week!"

With that she was gone, through the oak-panelled door. Which was kind of awkward for Mr Carter and Ryan, who were left there, not quite knowing what to do.

Eventually, Ryan coughed and said, "OK, yes.

Well. There we are. Goodbye, then."

"Yeah," said Mr Carter. "Bye."

And the two of them shuffled out.

CHAPTER 38

PS BUMBUMBUM

After Mr Carter, Dionna and Ryan had left Oakcroft, nothing happened for a bit. They thought that maybe Mrs Valentine-Fine OBE had decided not to pick up the challenge.

But then a message came through to the school by email.

This was it:

To: HeadTeacher@BracketWoodSchool.com

From: MrsValentineFineOBE@Oakcroft.edu

Dear Mr Carter,

It was very kind of you to come to my office yesterday and challenge our school to a debate. We have considered it and our answer is yes. Our only stipulation is that the motion should be:

This House Believes that Bracket Wood School is Rubbish.

Our school will be proposing the motion and you will be opposing it. I hope this is suitable for your purposes.

Yours truly,

Mrs Valentine-Fine OBE

After he read this, Mr Carter thought about writing back a very rude message indeed. (It occurred to him that since he was now, as far as most people knew, a grown-up, he could use some very grown-up swear words without anyone telling him off.) However, he talked it over with Dionna, who said, "Yeah, you're right, they're just taking the mickey – even more reason to wipe the floor with them!"

So, with her looking over his shoulder, he wrote back, saying:

To: MrsValentineFineOBE@Oakcroft.edu

From: HeadTeacher@BracketWoodSchool.com

Dear Mrs Valentine-Fine OBE,

Thanks for your email. Yeah. OK. That motion is fine. More than fine. Brilliant.

Yours sincerely,

Mr Carter

PS BUMBUMBUMBUMBUMBUMBUMBUM BUMBUMBUMBUMBUMBUMBUMBUMBUM BUMBUMBUMBUMBUMBUMBUMBUMBUM.

PPS Sorry, I think my computer has been hacked. By your mum.

Dionna did think about saying to him *Might be better if you cut the PS and the PPS*, but then thought, *Naaah*.

They laughed a lot, and carried on laughing right up until they realised that they would have to stage some auditions to find a second member of the Debating Team apart from Dionna.

CHAPTER 39
That Bad

"**T**his House believes . . ."

"My house? My house doesn't believe anything. It's made of brick."

Dionna looked despairingly at Mr Carter, who looked back and tried to smile as if things were not so bad. But it did look as if things were pretty bad. Morris Fawcett was the fifteenth child who'd come in following the putting up of a sign in the corridor that said:

Debating Team Auditions, 1.15pm.

And it wasn't going well.

"No, Morris," said Dionna. "It's not your actual house."

"Well, why did you say it was?"

"I didn't. I said, 'This House'."

"Oh." Morris frowned and looked around. "It's not a house, though. It's a school."

Dionna put her head in her hands.

Mr Carter said, "OK, thanks, Morris. We'll let you know."

"You'll let me know what?"

"Just go."

Morris nodded as if he'd heard these words often, and did so.

"What are we going to do?" said Dionna after the door had shut.

"Well, he isn't the cleverest pupil in the school."

"You can say that again."

"Well, he isn't the clever—"

"Please don't do that joke."

"No, fair enough. But some of the others haven't been that bad."

Dionna looked down at the notes she'd been taking.

"Scarlet and Stirling: have created a debate app that could do it for us. When asked, will it be ready by Monday, they replied, 'No, we are waiting for legal permission, which won't come through until we are sixteen.' In nine years' time for Stirling."

"Yes, but—"

"Malcolm Bailey: very good on impressions of animals. Not so good at debating."

"Hmm."

"Alfie Moore: seems to think he can win just by shouting, 'I'll do what I like!'"

"Yes, that was odd."

"Caspar, Reception: mainly interested in singing 'The Wheels on the Bus'." She looked up. "I've written *possible* and a question mark next to him. Things are *that* bad."

"Yeah. OK. You're right. They've all been terrible. The debate is on Monday. That's when OFFHEAD is coming back. And today is Friday. What are we going to do?"

She shook her head.

Then the door opened and through the door came Ryan. "How's it going?" he said.

Mr Carter and Dionna looked at each other.

And smiled.

CHAPTER 40

A Bit of a Problem

"I'm still not sure about this," said Ryan as he and Dionna waited in a little room behind the assembly-hall stage on Monday afternoon.

"Oh, not now, Mr Carter," she replied. "We've been over this."

And they had. Ryan – or rather, Mr Carter-inside-Ryan – had been very against the idea. The idea, that is, of him being the second player on the Bracket Wood Debating Team, which had occurred to Dionna and Mr Carter simultaneously as he'd walked through the door.

His point was that it was cheating. That he, though presently occupying the body of an eleven-year-old boy, was actually a forty-three-year-old man – a very strict, play-by-the-rules forty-three-year-old head teacher, in fact – and so he was not comfortable with the idea that they would have an unfair advantage.

Dionna had answered by looking up the rules of debating, which, it was true, contained nothing about a member of a school team being an adult in reality.

Mr Carter (in Ryan's body) countered that the age limit was twelve.

Ryan (in Mr Carter's body) countered that he, Ryan, was eleven.

Mr Carter (you get the idea) replied, "Yes, but I'm actually *me*. Mr Carter."

And Ryan had said, "Well, Mr C, I think there's a little bit of all of us in all of us."

"What's that supposed to mean?" said Mr Carter (in Ryan's body).

"Yes, what does it mean?" said Dionna. "Is it a Taylor Swift lyric?"

"Well, OK, maybe I wasn't really thinking what it meant when I said it," said Ryan (in Mr Carter's body). "But –" he continued, looking very closely at the body that had previously been his – "I am beginning to wonder where I start and you end. Whether we aren't just turning into each other."

When he'd said this, both of them felt a little frightened. So maybe, just to ward off the idea that this was it, that Mr Carter and Ryan had swapped places permanently, Mr Carter – in Ryan's voice, obviously – said, "OK, OK. I'll be on the debating team."

Which might be why he was now saying he

wasn't sure about it. After all, it wasn't a very strong argument. Which is a bit of a problem when you're about to take part in a debate.

CHAPTER 41
Shirley OBE

"**W**ell, Mr Carter, I have to say we are quite impressed," said Mr Mann, taking his seat in the front row of the assembly hall. The whole school sat behind them, waiting.

"Yes," said Miss Malik, who had her notebook out. "Look at what I've ticked. Food. Behaviour (in class, playground and corridor). Teaching."

"Thank you," said Mr Barrington, who was sitting behind.

"I wasn't sure about him, actually," whispered Miss Malik, "but everyone else was fine."

"Toilets?" said Mr Carter.

"Even toilets."

"I'd be happy to use them myself," said Mr Mann. "Well, not *happy*, as I'd have to squat in a very uncomfortable way and frankly my legs aren't what they were. But clean as a whistle."

"Well . . . great," said Mr Carter.

"But obviously," Mr Mann continued, "that just brings you up to scratch. What we're looking for, always, is that little bit extra!"

Mr Carter nodded enthusiastically, knowing that's what the real Mr Carter would have been doing in the circumstances.

"Yes," he said. "And that's why, to really show how Bracket Wood has improved since last time, we thought we'd organise this – a debate!"

"A debate!" said Miss Malik, writing it down in

her notebook. "What a good idea."

"Thank you! Would you mind being the judges?"

"Not at all."

"Indeed not," said Mr Mann. "I love a debate! Excellent! What's the motion?"

"Er . . ." said Mr Carter, pointing at the stage where a banner hung saying:

THIS SCHOOL IS RUBBISH!

"Oh . . ." said Mr Mann.

"Oh . . ." said Miss Malik.

"Yes, it occurs to me just now, for the first time," said Mr Carter, "that from your point of view that isn't a very helpful motion. But – you know – we'll be speaking against it, obviously."

"I see," said Miss Malik. "Well, I suppose if you win, that'll be all to the good."

"Hm," said Mr Mann. "Against whom are you debating?"

"Oak—" Mr Carter began.

"MR MANN! MISS MALIK! HOW WONDERFUL TO SEE YOU AGAIN! PARTICULARLY AFTER YOU JUST GAVE US OUR FIFTH RANKING IN A ROW OF OUTSTANDING!"

Mr Carter looked up from his seat to see Mrs Valentine-Fine OBE standing in front of the OFFHEAD inspectors with outstretched arms.

Behind her stood Belinda, Toby and a large group of immaculately uniformed Oakcroft pupils.

"Mrs Valentine-Fine OBE!" said Mr Mann, getting up.

"PLEASE. CALL ME SHIRLEY."

"Shirley!"

"BUT STILL OBE!"

"Sorry, OBE."

"AND SO GOOD THAT YOU'RE HERE! AFTER ALL, I REMEMBER BACK IN 1977 WHEN YOU – BRIAN – WERE CAPTAIN OF OUR DEBATING TEAM!"

"Oh, Shirley OBE. I thought you'd have forgotten!"

And Mr Mann gave Mrs Valentine-Fine OBE an enormous hug.

"—croft," finished Mr Carter. But no one really heard him.

CHAPTER 42

You'll Be Sorry

"Oh, blimey," said Mr Carter, coming into the backstage area, "I think things might be more difficult than we expected out there!"

"And not just out there," said Dionna, pointing at Ryan. "He's been saying he's not sure about being on the team again."

"No!"

"Which, frankly, neither am I."

"What?"

"I'm frightened," she said. "I just looked out and I know I faced them down when we were in Mrs Valentine-Fine—"

"OBE," said Mr Carter and Ryan together.

"Whatevs . . . When we were in her office, but that girl Belinda – she was the worst."

"The worst what?"

"The worst bully! To me! When I was there. And turns out her and that posh boy Toby *are* Oakcroft's debating team!"

"OK . . . well—"

"It's *not* OK. Just looking out there and seeing them smirking – it's making me really nervous! I don't know if I can do it, Ryan!"

"Yes, well, don't ask me to help," said Ryan. "As you know, I have my own issues."

"I think she's talking to me," said Mr Carter.

"Oh. Right," said Ryan. Dionna had retreated into the corner and was sobbing gently. Mr Carter looked over at her helplessly.

"Well . . ." said Ryan, coming close to him, and speaking quietly, "you know the thing you said about us turning into each other?"

Mr Carter nodded.

"I hope – for both our sakes – it isn't happening. But! If it turns out that you have indeed picked up a tiny bit of maturity – a tiny bit of head actual teacher-ishness from me –" he glanced behind him at Dionna – "you should be able to deal with this situation."

With that, he moved out of the way. Mr Carter looked at Dionna, still sobbing. He gulped and went over to her.

"Listen . . . Dee. You can do this. I know you can."

"How do you know?" she asked through a constricted throat.

"Because I know you. I know you had a terrible time at Oakcroft, but the fact that you left there doesn't mean they won. And you can show them that now, today. Because I know you're really brave."

"Am I?"

"Yeah. You've always been my right-hand girl. Whatever the prank. Remember when we put the bucket of frogs over the classroom door? It was up to you to make a lot of noise so that Barrington came barrelling in without looking up. And you gave it everything!"

Dionna laughed at this, even though she was still crying.

"Or that time we went to the library and asked for books with funny names. You went straight up there and asked the librarian for *Big Pants* by Hugh Jass!"

Dionna laughed more.

"And you asked for *Fifty Yards to the Toilet* by Willy Makit!" she said.

"I did!"

"And Mr Chumley spent ages looking for it in his cards!"

"Um . . ." said Ryan, coming over, "I'm not sure this is what I meant by . . . maturity."

Mr Carter and Dionna looked at each other.

"Well, it's done the trick!" she said. "Let's get out there and smash it!"

"Yeah!" said Mr Carter. And they were just about to go out on to the stage of the assembly hall when there was a bleeping noise.

"What's that?" said Mr Carter.

"It's my phone," said Ryan.

"Is it?"

"Yes."

Mr Carter started patting his suit.

"Where is it?"

"My inside pocket. That's where I always keep it."

"Do I?"

"Yes. I do."

Mr Carter reached into his inside pocket and took out the phone. At which point, Ryan grabbed it.

"Hey!" said Mr Carter. "It's *my* phone!"

Mr Carter looked at it in Ryan's hand. It was a very sensible one, only just a smartphone, with not even a cool cover or anything.

"Yes, it clearly is," he said. But Ryan didn't say anything. He was reading a text. When he looked up, his face did not look pleased.

"You went to St Winifred's?" he said sharply.

"Um. Yes. How do you—"

"Because this is a message saying that –" he checked it again – "my mother hopes I will come and visit her again soon. Because she is getting weaker all the time."

"Oh," said Mr Carter, "I'm really sorry."

"It also says . . ." and here Ryan frowned hard at the screen, "that the last visit from me . . . by which it means you, of course . . . was really special, and it meant more to her than . . ." – he paused, reading the words slowly – "any . . . other . . . visit . . . before." Ryan seemed to take a while to absorb these last words. Then he looked up. His face had gone very hard. "Well. There we are," he said, talking, it seemed, to himself.

"Listen, Mr C," said Mr Carter. "I . . ." But then he realised he didn't really know what to say. There was a very awkward silence.

Then, finally, Ryan spoke, through very tight lips. "Why did you do that? Go and visit her? She's *my* mother."

Mr Carter looked down. He did have some reasons,

but he didn't know whether or not they would make any difference to Ryan's anger. Which was scaring him. He might have the bigger body, but at the moment he was shrinking inside it.

Mr Carter just shrugged and continued to look down. A person watching from afar might have thought it odd that the head teacher, the grown-up in the suit, was acting like a told-off kid, while the boy in the school uniform was doing the telling-off.

"WHEN OH WHEN OH WHEN IS THIS SO-CALLED DEBATE GOING TO BEGIN?" came a loud and OBE-garlanded voice from inside the assembly hall.

"Well, we could just assume that the lateness of the Bracket Wood team is point one of our argument, couldn't we, Toby?" came another.

"Yuh, too right, Belinda. Cool idea."

"Come on!" hissed Dionna, walking over to the two of them. "Let's get out there!"

She walked on to the stage. Mr Carter finally

looked up, to see Ryan still staring at him.

"You'll be sorry for this, Ryan Ward. You'll be so, so sorry," he said, and then walked out after Dionna.

CHAPTER 43
Dregs

"To sum up, this House's argument is clear. This school, Jacket Food Comprehensive, is – one – a school that has continually scored poorly on its –" and at this point Belinda, who had been proposing the motion for some time, curtsied towards Mr Mann and Miss Malik – "OFFHEAD reports. And – two – is not getting any better. Recently, the school has just been in a terrible state. There have been stories of chaos in classrooms and corridors, of confectionery – confectionery! – being doled out at lunchtime, of homework being cancelled and of teacher shortages, with classes having to be taught by Reception children!"

Mr Carter wanted to raise his hand here, and say *Point of order! That wasn't because of a teacher shortage! I just did it because I thought it'd be funny! Which it was!* but there was no point in him doing so as he was sitting in the audience, and not actually on the debating team. And also it wouldn't have helped very much. So he just had to sit and watch as Belinda strode confidently forward to the front of the stage.

In the hall, the Bracket Wood pupils sat – the older ones on chairs, the younger ones in front, cross-legged. Lining the walls, though, were the visiting boys and girls from Oakcroft. Onstage, six seats had been set out opposite each other.

The left-hand side was Team Oakcroft. Belinda, until she had begun her speech, had been sitting there with Toby. On the right-hand side, presently looking a bit glum, sat Dionna and Ryan. In between were Mr Mann and Miss Malik. Above them hung the

THIS SCHOOL IS RUBBISH!

banner. The phrase seemed to gleam more strongly with every word that came out of Belinda's mouth.

"And – three . . . well," she said, moving her face slowly from side to side and doing the smirk that seemed to be her default expression, "just look around you. I don't wish to be rude . . ."

Don't you? thought Mr Carter (that's Ryan inside Mr Carter, btw).

". . . but really."

In the hall, the Bracket Wood children did what she asked. Barry Bennett looked at his friends Jake, Lukas and Taj, and then to Ellie Stone, who was looking at her brother Fred, who looked beyond her at Malcolm Bailey, who was looking over at Sam Green,

who was frowning at Alfie Moore, who was glancing at Stirling and Scarlet, who were looking at each other, although sitting in between them was a Year Five boy called Prajit who smelt slightly of Whiskas, and he was looking at Isla Fawcett, who was looking at her brother Morris, who had his eyes shut because he was asleep.

They all (apart from Morris, obviously) had an expression on their face that said, *Oh. Maybe she's right*.

"And then," Belinda continued, "look at us. Myself and Toby, the representatives of *Oakcroft* School." She said *Oakcroft* with special reverence as if she was saying the word *royal*. She gestured with both hands towards herself as if opening a pair of invisible curtains just in front of her. "Look at our clothes. Our bearing. Our natural confidence, intelligence and class." She went and smirked next to Toby, who stood up with her. "This is what schoolchildren should look like. Should simply, in fact, be. *We* are what a school that is definitely not rubbish breeds – a superior race . . ."

In the audience, Mrs Valentine-Fine OBE made a tiny gesture with her index finger, a gesture that meant *Not that, Belinda – bit too far.*

"Sorry, scratch that," said Belinda, hardly pausing for breath. "A superior *model* of pupil. A model pupil, if you will. As opposed to –" she looked across to where the Bracket Wood team was sitting and fixed her eye particularly on Dionna – "a rubbish pupil." Remarkably, as she said this, her smirk broke into a full smile. She turned back, still smiling, to the audience.

"Standing before you, I thus commend this motion to the gracious OFFHEAD judges. Thank you very much."

There was a small silence, followed by a burst of loud applause from where Mrs Valentine-Fine OBE was sitting.

"BRAVO! BRAVO! ENCORE! HEAR HEAR!" At which point, the Oakcroft group round the walls joined in, clapping and shouting, "Yes! Great job, Belly! Well done! You go, girl!" and suchlike.

Belinda sat down with a very strong sense of *sorted*. Miss Finch leant over from behind Mr Carter and said quietly, "Well, that was very irritating. But delivered supremely confidently. Which probably counts for quite a lot . . . ?"

"Maybe," replied Mr Carter, looking over at Miss Malik, who was scribbling furiously in her notebook. "But Dionna's great." He wanted to say, *And Ryan's actually forty-three years old, so that'll help*. But managed to suppress the urge. "Plus, the posh boy has to do his speech first. And I don't think he'll be as good as Belinda."

"Thank you very much, Belinda, the captain of Oakcroft's team," said Miss Malik. "And now, Toby, to second the motion, please."

Toby stood up, his long shaggy hair falling across his eyes. He put his hands in his pockets and ambled forward.

"Yuh. Well. What Bells said. Literally. I mean, this school, like, is clearly *so* basic. It's just dregs, and us Oaky boys and girls – we're clearly, like, on fleek. So you know – vote for us." And with that he smiled, clicked his tongue, winked and pointed with both index fingers at the audience.

"You see?" whispered Mr Carter, looking back at Miss Finch. "That won't have got Oakcroft many poi—"

But then he stopped whispering. Because he noticed that Miss Finch wasn't listening. She was just looking dreamily at Toby, who was still standing in his pose, smiling his very white-toothed smile.

Then he looked around and saw that every single girl and female teacher – and quite a few of the boys and men — were staring in more or less the same way at Toby.

Another big round of applause broke out all over the hall, during which Mr Carter noticed that joining in with the applause, and very much also doing the dreamy stare, was OFFHEAD inspector and debating judge Miss Malik.

CHAPTER 44
Stupid Old Oakcroft

"Miss Malik?" said Mr Mann after the applause finished.

"Hm?" she said, still staring at Toby.

"Time to do the next bit?"

"What? Oh. Yes . . ." she said, still smiling at Toby. "Well, it's been great so far. Spellbinding, really." She turned to look at team Bracket Wood. Dionna and Ryan were waiting. Neither of them seemed confident – Dionna looked nervous and Ryan sulky.

"So," said Miss Malik, "now it's the turn of Bracket Wood. And the first speaker is – Dionna Baxter!"

She applauded, every so often glancing at Toby, who had finally broken his pose and gone to sit down. There was a little bit of applause and some uncertain cheers from the home crowd in the hall.

Dionna stood up. In her right hand, she held some notes written on a series of cards. She coughed nervously, bringing that hand to her mouth quickly, which meant all those cards collided with her face and then spilt on to the floor.

"Oh!" she said. "Sorry."

There were some laughs from the Oakcroft pupils in the hall, and two, very pointedly, from the Oakcroft area of the stage.

Dionna began to pick up the cards, but they were made of the sort of paper that sticks easily to a surface, and after trying to get one up for nearly ten seconds she sighed, shook her head and gave up.

"Oh, never mind," she said. "I know what I want to say anyway."

She faced forward and moved to the front of the stage.

"They're right in some ways, aren't they?" she said, addressing the hall, but gesturing towards Belinda and Toby. "Pupils at this school will probably never be as well-spoken and beautifully put together as . . . Belly and Tobes."

A ripple of laughter went through the crowd at the way Dionna said the posh nicknames. Belinda sniffed and looked away as if hardly listening. Toby flicked his hair out of his eyes. Again.

"And probably, if your only mark of whether this is a good primary school is how many children make it into a posh secondary school – well, again, I suppose Oakcroft is going to win every time."

At the front of the audience, Mrs Valentine-Fine OBE nodded enthusiastically.

"SHE'S DOING WELL. FOR US!" she said in the nearest thing she could to a whisper, which was more like a very breathy shout.

"But there are other things," continued Dionna, "that make a school a good school. Number one, I would say, is *happiness*. Maybe Mrs Valentine-Fine—"

"OBE!"

"—wouldn't put that very high on the list, but, you see, I have a unique – for those of you in Reception and Years One and Two, that means I'm the only one – viewpoint as regards this debate. Because even though the debate isn't about whether Oakcroft is a better school than Bracket Wood, Belinda, and to a lesser extent, Toby, have *made* it about that. Bracket Wood, they're saying, is clearly rubbish because Oakcroft is so much better. But my unique position is that I've been a pupil at both schools. I went to Oakcroft and now I'm here. And I can't even begin to tell you how much happier I am here."

A murmur went round the hall – of excitement, of surprise, of the tables being turned.

"My parents – and I – were very excited when I got into Oakcroft. It is supposed to be the best school in the area, and kids like me aren't meant to go to places like that. But the trouble was – that's how I was made to feel all the time. Like someone who wasn't meant to be there. By some of the staff, even, from time to time. But *all* the time by some of the pupils . . ."

She looked over meaningfully at Belinda. Who tried to sniff and look away again, but since she'd been looking away to begin with, that meant she had to look away even more. Which was a bad idea, as it involved swinging her face almost completely behind her.

"Ow!" said Belinda.

"What is it, Bells?" asked Toby.

"I've cricked my neck!"

"But," said Dionna, "let's not even go there. I don't want to win this debate by asking for your pity. Or by going on about what happened in the past at that school. I want to talk about how much I like it now, here, at this school. Because, let's be honest, everybody. School. It's boring. It's not meant to be fun. Bits of it can be, though. It can be because if it's a place where you feel safe and there are no bullies, then in between the boring bits you can have fun."

And here she looked directly at Mr Carter, sitting there willing her to win and to carry on speaking so well.

"Fun with your friends. I love this school and I think it is a good school because it's friendly. I have made good, real, lovely friends here. And that's why I'd rather be here than stupid old Oakcroft any day!"

Dionna went and sat down. Mr Carter watched her. For the second time that month, a person who'd known the head teacher for a while might have been surprised to see a tear appear in his eye and roll down his cheek. But the tear was accompanied, this time, by a big smile and an equally big thumbs-up in her direction.

She saw it and smiled back.

At which point, the hall broke out into thunderous applause. There was clapping and cheering and stamping of feet. From the Bracket Wood children (and staff), of course, although Toby joined in until Belinda slapped him.

"Oh, right. Soz," he said.

"Well," said Mr Mann, getting up from his central chair. "That was a very impressive speech from the Bracket Wood captain, I must say. Which has made the match rather closer than perhaps we all thought it would be . . . and means that everything, I think, is resting on the final speech, which will be coming from Bracket Wood's seconder – Ryan Ward!"

A hush descended on the hall. All eyes went to the second chair on the Bracket Wood side. And then Ryan, who had been looking down for most of Dionna's speech, looked up.

CHAPTER 45
A Job Well Done

As Ryan got up to speak, Mr Barrington turned to Mr Carter and whispered, "Er . . . Headmaster . . . Ryan Ward? Really?"

Miss Finch leant over and added, "Yes. Are we sure about this?"

And Mrs Wang said, "Oh no. Not him."

Even Miss Gerard, who'd turned up late and seemed to have had her eyes shut for most of the debate, murmured, "Well, that's that; then."

"No!" said Mr Carter to all of them. "It's going to be fine! You'll see. You may not have noticed . . . but Ryan's, well –" and here he smiled confidently – "he's acquired a certain maturity recently." Still smiling, he looked back to the stage and folded his arms. "I think, members of staff, that you are about to see that maturity in action. Right now."

The staff all turned to look. Ryan Ward came to the front of stage. He stroked his chin. He frowned. And then spoke as if he was setting out an argument very carefully.

"Bum. Poo. Willy."

There was a short pause. Then he said, a bit louder, "Willy! Poo! Bum!" Then, raising a finger in the air as if he was developing a serious argument, "Willy, willy, willy? Poo? Bum? Fart! But there must be other issues, you say? Well, yes, there are."

"Um . . ." whispered Mr Carter to the rest of the teachers, who were watching open-mouthed, "maybe he's just warming up."

"Pants!"

"Oh."

"Pants, pants, pants, pants, pants. And kaka. Bum chocolate! Of course."

The open-mouthed look was now shared by Dionna, Belinda, Toby, Mrs Valentine-Fine OBE and everyone else in the assembly hall. Except for Years One to Four, who were laughing hysterically. Some of their mouths *were* open, obviously.

"What else is there to say? Snot, I suppose. Knickers. And some would say, although I wouldn't necessarily support this myself, wee-wee." He paused as if reaching a conclusion. "And so, ladies and gentlemen, children, honoured judges, of course, I think I can sum up everything I've been arguing in this debate, by just saying . . ."

And here he stuck his tongue out and went:

"BLLLLLLLRRRLLLRRRLRRRRRRLLLRRRRRRLL RRRRBBBRRLLLLLLLLRRRRRRRRR!"

It was possibly the biggest, loudest and longest raspberry anyone in that hall had ever heard. And with that Ryan Ward nodded, as you might after thinking *That's a job well done*, walked off the stage and left the assembly hall.

CHAPTER 46
OMG

"Well!" said Mr Mann, getting up. "I suppose that ends the debate. Bit unexpected, that last speech. Well. I don't know that we really have to spend much time thinking about who the winner is, do we, Miss Malik? I mean, honestly?"

Mr Carter looked over, desperately trying to catch the eye of Dionna. But she was just looking depressed.

"I HARDLY THINK SO!"

"No, absolutely, Mrs Valentine-Fine OBE. So. The winner of the debate, and indeed of the argument as to whether or not 'This School is Rubbish!', is, of course . . ."

"Hold on!" said Miss Malik.

Mr Mann frowned. "Sorry?"

"I said hold on a minute. You're forgetting that the girl's speech – Dionna's – was very good indeed."

"Well," said Mr Mann, "I'm not forgetting that. I just think its effect was cancelled out somewhat by the seconder's speech. Which if you remember was mainly just some rude words."

"ABSOLUTELY!"

"Quite right!" said Belinda.

"Yuh!" said Toby.

"Yes, but Oakcroft's seconder just said some posh stuff! That didn't really make any sense either!"

"Well . . ." said Mr Mann, looking between her and Toby, who seemed a little miffed, "you appeared to be enjoying it at the time."

"Yes! He's very . . . neat and tidy. Well done. But at the end of the day, we are here to judge how these children put their arguments together, and deliver their speeches. And on this, I'd say both first speeches were strong. Even if the Oakcroft one betrayed more than a little snobbery . . . "

A confused glance passed between Belinda and Mrs Valentine-Fine OBE at this, as if they weren't quite sure what the word "snobbery" might mean.

"'Standing before you, I commend this motion, though," said Mr Mann, quoting Belinda. "That's a very good use of the fronted adverbial . . . "

"Perhaps. Meanwhile, both second speeches . . . well. They were both a little surprising, let's put it like that."

Mr Mann frowned, and nodded. "Well. What would you suggest, then?"

Miss Malik frowned, but then Mr Carter suddenly got up and walked on to the stage.

"A draw?" he said.

Miss Malik and Mr Mann looked at each other.

"Hmm . . ." said Mr Mann. "Just give us a moment to discuss this, please."

He ushered Miss Malik off to the wings of the stage, where they began whispering to each other.

Meanwhile, Mr Carter heard a voice, also whispering.

"Ryan!"

He ignored it. It had been so long since anyone had called him Ryan that he assumed it was someone seeing Ryan coming back into the hall.

"Ryan!" said the voice again, more insistent.

"Oh!" he said, realising that it was Dionna talking to him. He went over to her. She was looking very worried.

"A draw won't be good enough," she whispered.

"What do you mean?" he whispered back. "It's a

good result, considering everyone thought Oakcroft was going to win anyway."

"Oh, you're such a numpty. The result of the debate doesn't matter by itself! What matters is the rating the OFFHEAD inspectors give the school. And we all know that we needed to win the debate for them to give us a good rating."

"Oh . . . Yeah."

"Why did Mr Carter just say all those rude words?"

Ryan shook his head. "I think he was a bit . . . upset . . . about his mum. I'm not sure."

Dionna knitted her brow. "I wish he hadn't— Oh! They're coming back."

Mr Carter looked round. They were approaching with expressions on their faces that said *We have come to a decision*.

"OK, well, maybe we can show them something else – apart from the debate – that will convince them to up the rating?"

"Oh yes, right. Maybe Morris Fawcett's brain will swap places with Brian Cox's."

"Well. Mine swapped with Mr Carter's."

"Ryan."

"Dionna. I don't know what to say. What else can I do to show them we're a good school?"

"So!" said Mr Mann. "We have deliberated and cogitated, as someone once said."

"Get on with it!" came a shout from the audience – a Bracket Wood shout unfortunately. Mr Carter – and Dionna – grimaced.

"Well. Ahem, OK," said Mr Mann. "Our decision is, as Mr Carter suggests, that the result is a draw."

"OMG, I CANNOT BELIEVE IT!"

"I'm sorry, Mrs Valentine-Fine OBE, but our decision is final. And we think that is a fair result."

"Yes!" said Mr Carter, stepping in. "It is. Excellent judgement from . . . the judges! Could we have a round of applause?"

The hall applauded. Mr Carter moved forward, bringing the OFFHEAD inspectors with him, one on either side. All he could think to do was to delay them, keep them happy, in the hope that they would give Bracket Wood a better rating.

"Come on, everybody, let's hear it for Mr Mann and Miss Malik!"

The applause carried on.

"Yes, thank you, Mr Carter," said Miss Malik. "That's very nice to hear, but we really must be going."

"Give it up, for M and M!"

"Really, Mr Carter!" said Mr Mann. "Thank you, but as my colleague says, we have a busy day ahead, inspecting other schools!"

"Hip hip hOFFHEAD!"

"RIGHT, WE'RE LEAVING! TIME TO GO BACK TO CIVILISATION AFTER THIS TRAVESTY!" shouted Mrs Valentine-Fine OBE,

coming on to the stage. "COME ON, BELINDA!
TOBY!"

They got up and followed her. But Mr Carter
wasn't watching them and wasn't listening to the
OFFHEAD inspectors' protestations. He was lost
about what to do now, and thought shouting and
cheering would somehow help. So he pushed the
inspectors even further forward in front of him and
shouted, "Yes! Wooo wooo wooo! Yay, OFFHEAD!
You're the best!"

It wasn't working. Mr Mann and Miss Malik merely
looked embarrassed. More embarrassed, indeed,
because Mr Carter had just pushed them into Mrs
Valentine-Fine OBE and Toby and Belinda, who
were trying to leave the stage at the same time. It
was embarrassing for everyone; everyone was going
pink in the face.

But actually not just in the face. All over.
From head to foot. Because suddenly Mr Mann,

Miss Malik, Mrs Valentine-Fine OBE, Belinda and
Toby were covered in a huge dump from above of
cake-mix stew.

CHAPTER 47
A Very Strong Word

For a moment, no one said anything. For a moment, there was just silence as the cloud of pink powder thrown up by the cake-mix-stew dump settled, and the five completely gunked people on stage just stood there in shock.

And then they all started shouting at once. "URGGGGGHHHHH!"

"WHAT IS IT?"

"I CAN'T SEE MY NOTEBOOK!"

"MY HAIR! MY LOVELY HAIR!"

"I'M BLEEDING! I'M BLEEDING!"

"NO, YOU'RE NOT, MRS VALENTINE-FINE!"

"OBE!"

"SORRY, OBE!"

"WHO DID THIS?" shouted Mr Mann – louder, even, than Mrs Valentine-Fine OBE.

It was a good question. And the answer was fairly quick to reveal itself.

Mr Carter and Dionna (and all the teachers and indeed the whole audience) were looking up. Above the assembly-hall stage, used sometimes for school plays, was a series of rafters on which to hang curtains and scenery. Climbing down from these, holding two big metal containers dripping with the remains of what had clearly been a LOT of cake-mix stew, and smiling – beaming, in fact – was Ryan Ward.

"I did!" he said, jumping down the final bit to the stage.

"Ryan Ward!" said Mr Barrington.

"The very same," said Ryan, turning to the audience proudly. "I am, yes, Ryan Ward, the best prankster in the history of Bracket Wood School!"

A round of applause broke out.

"STOP THAT!" shouted Mr Mann.

"Yes . . . maybe . . . *do* stop it," said Mr Carter.

"What are you going to do about this, Mr Carter?" said Miss Malik, wiping her face with a tissue. It wasn't helping much.

"YES, WHAT?"

Mr Mann, Miss Malik, Mrs Valentine-Fine OBE, Toby and Belinda were all glaring at him. Their looks were made more aggressive because all Mr Carter could see of their faces were their eyes staring out of the pink mess. He turned round. The whole school was looking at him as well. *What would a real head* teacher do in this situation? he thought. *Oh well, there's only one way to find out.*

"First," he said, grabbing hold of Ryan and pulling him offstage, "I'm going to have a strong word with this boy. A *very* strong word!"

CHAPTER 48

When You Say Guys

"**W**hy, Mr Carter?" said Mr Carter. "Why did you do it? Not just the cake mix, but the rude words in your speech? Why?"

They were standing just outside the hall in the corridor. Through the windows of the hall doors could be seen what looked like a series of cartoon characters onstage, a family of pink blobs, all standing and looking back at them, not able to hear what was being said.

Ryan was looking down. He was shaking his head. Then he looked up.

"Because, Ryan, up until an hour ago, I had started to think this whole weird experience might actually have been worth something. I thought it was teaching you something – and as a teacher that made it OK. I thought it was teaching you how to be a bit older, a bit more mature. But then when I found out you'd done something as stupid and immature as going to see my mother, I just thought, *It's all been a waste of time. What's the point? Might as well go the whole Ryan Ward hog and prank this thing to death.*"

Mr Carter frowned. "Just because I went to see your mum?"

"Yes! Because I don't want the last time my mother sees me for it not to be me!"

Mr Carter frowned more. "The last time . . . ?"

"Yes!"

Mr Carter frowned even more. "Is she . . . ?"

He didn't want to say it.

"Ryan," said Ryan. "She's in a hospice."

"I know. Well, I saw that's what it was called. But I don't know what that is. I just thought it was a type of hospital."

"No. It's a place for people who are—"

"Yes. I understand now."

Mr Carter went quiet for a bit. "I'm sorry. I'm really sorry," he said eventually. "But . . . I was lonely! And I missed my mum! And . . . I didn't like the thought of your mum being ill on her own!"

Ryan looked a bit taken aback by all these reasons suddenly tumbling out. "Well . . ." said Ryan. "But you should at least have told me you'd been to see her! That the hospice was calling!"

"Yes . . . you're right. Of course. But . . . I didn't know what a hospice was. Really. And even if I had, I wouldn't have known what to do." Mr Carter looked up, his eyes moist. "These are very big – very *grown-*

up – things to deal with, Mr Carter. And yes, I think I have grown up a bit. Like you said. But inside . . . I am still only eleven."

Ryan looked at him. He frowned. He shook his head. And then his own eyes softened a little. "OK. Yes. Maybe. Oh dear." He looked into the hall where the pink people were starting to look very impatient. "Maybe I went too far. I'm sorry, Ryan. I was angry with you. I was angry with everything, with the school, with this stupid being-in-the-wrong-body thing . . . And with my mother preferring a visit from you to a visit from me!"

"Yes, I can see that," said Mr Carter.

"Because I want to be there, for my mum. And I want to be there as me. Her forty-three-year-old son."

Ryan's eyes softened more, beginning to fill up with tears. It was him, in fact, not Mr Carter, who began to cry. It might not have looked that odd to people watching from inside the hall, that the told-off boy was starting to cry. But actually it was the first time the man inside the told-off boy had cried for a very, very long time.

Then the hall door opened. It was Dionna.

"Guys. You've got to come back inside. And clean up this mess. Somehow."

Mr Carter looked at her and then at the boy next to him, tears still running down his cheeks. His face set into a determined expression.

"When you say *guys*," he said, going past her, "I think you mean me."

CHAPTER 49

Not. At. All.

"Right, Mr Carter!" said Mr Mann, who had crossed his arms and was standing in a way that said *I may be covered in cake mix, but I am still a man of great importance.* "We have been waiting here for some time."

Mr Carter had come into the hall. Dionna had followed him in and, finally, looking sheepish, Ryan.

"I would say NONE of what has happened today reflects well on your school. And given how precarious Bracket Wood's OFFHEAD position has been over the last few years, I don't think you can blame anyone for whatever may happen when we submit our report. But putting that aside for the moment, what punishment – and I think Miss Malik and I will be very interested to observe this as it may be your last chance to save the situation – are you going to mete out to the boy who is responsible for . . ." and here Mr Mann swept a pink arm around in the direction of the entire stage ". . . this!"

Mr Carter stepped up on to the stage and stood in front of the five of them, all still dripping with cake mix. He had to dodge the puddles of it that had developed over the last few minutes.

"Come here, Ryan Ward!" he said.

Ryan looked at him, then shuffled slowly up the side stairs to the stage, also dodging the pink puddles, and stood next to Mr Carter. Then he looked at the floor again.

"So," said Mr Carter. "You ask me, Mr Mann, a very good question. And that is, what punishment am I going to give this boy, who has gunked all of you good people with cake-mix stew. So that you look like Peppa Pig's family."

The five pink people looked at each other. This wasn't quite what they expected. But he continued.

"That simply won't do because you are all very, very important people. So. I haven't actually been a head teacher that long, but during the short time that I've been in the job, I've learnt a few things. And the things I've learnt have led me to this decision. Which is . . . I am going to punish Ryan Ward . . . Not. At. All."

There was a short silence following this announcement. Then Mr Mann said, "Sorry, Mr Carter. I don't think I quite caught that."

"Didn't you? That's odd. Because I said it really slowly, spacing out all the words, like there was a full stop between each one. I'm going to punish him Not. At. All. By which I mean, he's not going to get a punishment."

CHAPTER 50

BAH!

All five gunked people looked completely stumped by this. Although, to be honest, they already looked quite stumped just by being covered in cake-mix stew. Ryan, looking up at last, looked quite surprised himself.

"Here's the thing," Mr Carter continued. "Ryan has been under a lot of . . . pressure recently. Things haven't been quite . . . right in his world for a little while. It's all been very topsy-turvy and confusing.

Hasn't it, Ryan?"

Ryan looked at him. Without any sarcasm, he answered in a small voice. "Yes."

"And on top of this, his mother is ill. Very ill. I don't want to talk about it too much – it's a private thing, of course – but I know it's been causing Ryan an awful lot of pain and he's very, very worried about her."

Silence fell upon the hall and the stage after he said this.

"Aren't you?"

"Yes," said Ryan in the same small voice.

"And sometimes when we're very, very worried about something we do stupid, angry things. Don't we?"

"Yes. Yes, Mr Carter," said Ryan.

Mr Carter nodded and turned back towards the stage, looking particularly at the two OFFHEAD inspectors.

"Look, I know that you're cross because you're covered in cake-mix stew, but you know what? Cake-mix stew will come off. What won't come off, I don't think, are really bad things happening to you."

There was a silence again here, but not a complete silence because in it could be heard a little murmuring – murmurs of agreement, of people in the room saying, "Yes" and, "That's right" and, "Good point".

"Because, Mr Mann, Miss Malik," continued Mr Carter, "I think we're all in the business – aren't we? – of trying to make life better for kids. And when life is tough for them the one thing I guess we should have is understanding. And maybe a bit of mercy. So that's why, because I know he's ashamed about what he did anyway, I am not going to punish Ryan Ward."

No one said anything for a tiny moment. And then, very, very slowly, a ripple of applause started at the back of the hall. It got louder and louder as all the children, the Oakcroft pupils as well as the Bracket Wood ones, joined in. It got louder still as they rose to their feet and began stamping and cheering.

And then Dionna, onstage, turned to the audience and began to sing, "OH! HEADMASTER CAR-TER!"

Mr Carter looked around and suddenly, *everyone* joined in.

"OH! HEADMASTER CAR-TER!"

Even the Oakcroft children. Even Miss Gerard and Mr Barrington. Even, as the head teacher looked round onstage, Miss Malik, and then, a bit more reluctantly and uncertainly as if he wasn't quite sure but finally decided to do it anyway, Mr Mann.

"OH! HEADMASTER CAR-TER!"

And even Ryan Ward.

"OH! HEADMASTER CAR— This is a bit weird, I have to tell you . . ." he said "—TER!"

Mr Carter smiled. There were three people who weren't doing it, of course.

"RIGHT, TOBY, BELINDA! THAT'S ENOUGH! LET'S GO!" one of those three people shouted. Still covered in the pink cake-muck, she, Toby and Belinda left the stage and made their way towards the door.

"Actually, Bells," said Toby, licking a finger, "it's surprisingly treats."

"Oh, shut up, you posh himbo!"

"Sorry about everything, Mrs Valentine-Fine!" called Mr Carter after them.

"OBE!"

"Which stands for OLD BATTLEAXE EEURGHH!"

They stopped in their tracks and turned round. Mrs Valentine-Fine OBE, if it was possible, looked more furious than ever.

"WHO SAID THAT?"

A hand went up quickly from a person onstage.

It was Ryan Ward.

Well, it was Mr Carter. Inside Ryan Ward. And he seemed very proud and pleased with himself.

Mr Carter, or the man who seemed to be Mr Carter, shrugged. He was clearly not going to punish Ryan Ward for that either. So Mrs Valentine-Fine OBE raised herself up to her not very full height, said, "BAH!" and left the assembly hall.

CHAPTER 51
Weird Music

"Ryan? Ryan? Can you hear me?"

A tiny blinking of the eyes indicated that he could.

"I think he's waking up."

"Ryan?"

Ryan opened his eyes. His mum, Tina, was there and Dionna, looking down at him. He was clearly in a bed. In fact, he was clearly in the same emergency room in the same hospital as two weeks ago when this whole thing had started.

"Oh, Ryan!" said his mum, and threw her arms round him. "What's happening with this fainting? I'm really worried about you!"

It was at this point that Ryan realised he wasn't, however, in the same *bed* as two weeks ago. He was in the opposite bed. Because he could see Mr Carter asleep in the facing bed. And it *was* Mr Carter. And he *was* Ryan. Which might also be why it felt quite nice and quite like coming home that Tina, his mum, was giving him a big hug.

MR. CARTER

"Mrs Ward? Can I have a word?" said the doctor. "It might be best just to let Ryan get used to the light for a bit; then you can come and talk to him."

His mum broke the hug, gave him a kiss on the forehead and moved away with the doctor.

At which point, Ryan turned to Dionna and said quietly, "What happened?"

"I need to know who you are first," she replied softly.

He frowned. "Why do you need to know that?"

"Because otherwise explaining what happened will be really confusing.

Because I'll be saying Mr Carter when I mean you and you when I mean Mr Carter. I mean, I'll probably be doing that anyway, but at least I'll know who I'm talking to."

"OK. Yes. I'm Ryan. I'm back in my own body. Which, I have to say, although I'm a bit groggy, feels much better. I don't recommend suddenly being forty-three, physically, at all. So what happened?"

"Well," she said. "After the debate, the OFFHEAD inspectors went and got cleaned up in the toilets."

"Thank heavens we sorted those out."

"Yes. And then me and you and Ryan – who at that point was really Mr Carter – went to his – your – oh, whatevs – the head teacher's office. Then we started talking about what had happened and whether or not it would be enough for us to get a good OFFHEAD rating. And while we were talking, this weird musical box that was on the head teacher's desk started playing its weird music. And then when

I looked round, both of you were lying asleep on the floor."

Ryan looked at her. "Thanks."

"What, for telling you all that?"

"No. Well, yes. But more for just being such a good friend. And also for smashing your bit of the debate. It was amazing."

She smiled at him. "It's good to have you back, Ryan," she said.

CHAPTER 52

Brother

One of the annoying things about coming out of hospital was that Ryan had just been in bed and now had to go to bed. This was partly because he'd come out in the evening and partly because the doctors had told his mum that he probably should get more rest, what with having had another one of these strange fainting moments they couldn't understand. That's what doctors prescribe when something they can't understand happens to someone – rest.

But he was pleased, having said that, to be back in his own bed. Not so much because of the one in hospital (in which he'd only been awake for a tiny bit anyway) but because of Mr Carter's, which had always been too big. Perhaps the weirdest thing about the whole experience – apart, obviously, from going to the toilet, which we're *still* not going to go into – was sleeping in his head teacher's bed.

"I'm sorry," said Tina, "I still haven't changed the duvet."

"Pardon?" said Ryan, sitting up, worried, as he'd have liked the duvet to have been washed since Mr Carter had slept in his bed. Then again, Mr Carter had also been sleeping in his body. So. There was clearly still a lot of processing to be done.

"'Uvet!" said Holly, who was on Tina's lap.

"Well, you've been saying for a while that this one, with all the pirates on the cover, is a bit young for you. Which I guess it is. I really felt that recently when you weren't feeling well and I tucked you in."

"You did?"

"Yes. I thought you felt too old now, for pirates."

"'Irates!" said Holly. "'Irates 'uvet!"

"Night-night, Ryan!" came a voice from outside the room. BAWOOOSHOO!

"Night-night, Aunt Annie," said Ryan. Then, as she walked away from the door, he added quietly, "Er . . . how long is she staying?"

"Just tonight. At least she didn't actually step *inside* the room."

FAGROOn!

"Yes . . ." said Ryan, smiling, at some level actually pleased to hear these sounds. It was all part of his family life, his familiar family life.

"So, anyway, I've been looking at a few other duvets. There's an all-black one you can get—"

"Mum," said Ryan, "I love this duvet."

She frowned. "Really?"

"Yes," he said, smiling. "And I love you."

Tina frowned again, harder. She was smiling as well because it was such a lovely thing for him to say, but she couldn't stop the frown deepening at the same time. Ryan *never* said that normally. Not unless she forced him to by saying it and staring at him until he had to reply in kind.

It made her wonder for a second about all the times recently that Ryan had been saying he *wasn't* Ryan. But then Holly reached up to her brother, touched his cheek and said, "Ryan. Yes. Ryan. My *brother*."

And both of them laughed and clapped because Holly had never said his whole name and got it right ever before.

CHAPTER 53

Is That All?

Ryan Ward sat anxiously outside the head teacher's office. He'd been here many times before, of course, but he had hoped that now things might be different. Mr Carter's assembly had been OK – he'd basically announced that things had been a little strange for a while, but now it was time to get everything back to normal. Then at the end of it he'd said quite sternly, "And, Ryan Ward! Come see me in my office after school."

So maybe it was all going to be boringly back to normal, with him just as much in trouble as ever. Maybe Mr Carter was just going to tell him off for all the things he'd done when he'd been head teacher.

Then Mr Carter opened the door.

"Hello, Ryan," he said. "Come in." Which Ryan did. And went to sit down opposite Mr Carter's desk.

"Look, Mr Carter," he said. "I'm really sorry about everything I did. When I was you, I mean. All the making Reception kids take classes and the *British Tortoise* game, and cancelling the homework and—"

"Are you well?" said Mr Carter.

"Pardon?"

"Well. You know. Everything . . . in its proper place. No ill effects. From our . . . experience?"

"Oh! Yeah. I'm fine. And, actually, I'm very pleased that when I go for a wee now I don't have to—"

"Yes, I think it's still best that we don't talk about that."

"Yes. OK."

"In fact, I'm not sure if we should really mention this – the whole body-swap *thing* – to anyone. Apart, obviously, from Dionna, who already knows. Because it might make us sound a bit . . ."

"Mad?" said Ryan.

"Hm," said Mr Carter.

There was a short pause then. Mr Carter frowned as if not sure what to say next. Ryan started to wonder when the big telling-off was coming.

"Also, Ryan, I just wanted to let you know a few things," said the head teacher eventually. "That I thought you might like to know. First of all . . . ah . . . They're here."

"Who is?" said Ryan, looking round. But Mr Carter had gone to the door and opened it. He was smiling a lot, for him. Ryan couldn't work out why until he saw his mum coming through the door in a wheelchair. Not *his* mum – Mr Carter's mum. Grace.

She was being pushed by Zadie the nurse.

"Hello, Mum," said Mr Carter softly.

"Hello, Michael," said Grace, smiling. She had a blanket over her knees and a needle in the back of her hand that was connected to a bag of liquid attached to the chair, but she looked happy.

Zadie pushed the chair in to the room and then wheeled it round so she was facing Mr Carter and Ryan.

"Wow!" said Ryan.

"Hello," said Grace. "Who are you?"

"This is Ryan Ward, Mum. He's one of our pupils here. Ryan, this is my mum, Grace."

"Yes. I kn—"

"And," continued Mr Carter, cutting him off, "my mum's not been very well, but recently she's got a bit better. It was unexpected."

He paused, then continued. "The doctors think that when I . . ." As he spoke, he looked closely at Ryan. "Yes, when I came to see her last time, it cheered her up a lot . . . the way I was."

"You cried!" said Grace, reaching out a hand to him. He took it and smiled at her.

"Yes. Apparently. I mean, it's a bit of a blur in my memory."

"Perhaps," said Ryan, smiling a little himself now, "because you were so . . . emotional?"

Mr Carter nodded. "Well, anyway, whatever happened, it helped my mother's state of mind and she's had at least a temporary reprieve."

"Hello? Everybody?" said Grace. "I *am* still here."

"You see," said Zadie, looking at Mr Carter. "Right back to her normal self!"

"Sorry, Mum."

"That's all right, Michael. I just wanted to see the school. It's lovely!"

Mr Carter and Ryan exchanged glances. Ryan's glance said, quite clearly, *I thought you said she was much better. But now she's said the school is lovely?*

"Yes," said Zadie. "But we need to get back. I told them we wouldn't be out for long."

Grace nodded and Zadie gripped the handles of her wheelchair. Grace looked up. Mr Carter knelt down and kissed her gently on the cheek. She closed her eyes. Then she opened them, held out her hand and said, "Very nice to meet you, Ryan."

Ryan took her hand. It was light as a feather. As they touched, she added, "And I hope we meet again. I wouldn't want this to be the *only* time we've met."

Ryan looked at her. She was smiling as if . . . as if she knew it wasn't. Ryan opened his mouth to reply, perhaps even to tell her it wasn't.

But then Zadie said, "Come on, Grace. Stop stalling." And pulled her backwards and out of the door. Ryan watched her go. Then he felt a hand on his shoulder. He looked up. Mr Carter was looking down at him.

"Thank you," he said.

Ryan turned to leave. "Is that all, Mr Carter?"

"No," said the head teacher. "Not quite. There's just one more thing."

CHAPTER 54
One More Thing

Ryan turned back.

"I just wanted to tell you something as well,"
continued Mr Carter. "You remember when we had
that – slightly heated – conversation just after you
told me you'd been to see my mother? And I – well, I
said how I thought this process was about teaching
you something? How to be a bit more grown-up?"

Ryan nodded. "I think it did," he said.

"Yes. But I think it was also teaching *me* something.

Which I didn't realise at the time."

"Which was what?" said Ryan.

Mr Carter looked thoughtful for a moment. Then he said, "How to be a bit *less* grown-up. Here's the thing, Ryan. Really, at heart, people my age – we're not grown-ups. We're just older children. Life forces us to behave in a very serious way a lot of the time, but inside most of us feel – well, about your age – about eleven. But I think I'd forgotten that however old you are, you don't have to spend all your time being *adult*."

"Right," said Ryan, nodding.

"I mean, don't get me wrong. Now that I'm back being me . . . I'm not going to introduce funny walks and shouting in the corridors. And when I was . . . you . . . when I did the prank with the cake stew on top of the inspectors . . . well, I realise now that was the child part, the immature part, taking over, going too far. So it's a balance, really, I suppose, and . . ."

As Mr Carter talked, Ryan looked out of the window, not really listening any more. Ryan *had* grown up a bit during this adventure. He even secretly quite liked this new relationship with Mr Carter, where Mr Carter was sort of like his dad, doing the sort of dad things his real dad never did – like teaching him important life lessons.

But Ryan could see his friends playing football in the playground now. And felt he'd like Mr Carter to stop with the important life lessons so he could get out there and join in.

"And one more thing I wanted to tell you," said Mr Carter, snapping Ryan's attention back to him. "Well. Not tell you. Share with you. One more thing I thought we should do together."

Mr Carter turned round. On his desk, next to the musical box, in fact, was an envelope. It was marked OFFHEAD.

CHAPTER 55
One More One-more Thing

"**Y**ou haven't opened it yet?" said Ryan.

"No. As I say, I wanted to share it with you, as I think whatever is in here, you are more than partly responsible for it."

"Hmm." Ryan got up and went to the window. "Not just me."

"What are you doing?" said Mr Carter.

"Opening the window."

"That one is always a bit stiff."

"Not if you twist it here, I noticed, when I was in this office – and then lift this handle a bit."

"Oh," said Mr Carter. "I never worked that out."

"Dionna!" shouted Ryan out of the open window. "Dee! Come here!"

"I'm playing football!"

"I know. Just for a moment!"

She raised her eyes to heaven, waved a "sorry" gesture at her playmates and ran over.

"What is it?" she said breathlessly.

"Mr Carter wants to share something with . . . us," said Ryan.

"Yes, of course," said Mr Carter, nodding. "You're right. This –" and he held up the OFFHEAD envelope – "should involve the three of us!"

"Oh, cripes!" said Dionna.

"Cripes?" said Ryan.

"I'm trying to avoid rude words," said Dionna.

"Probably best," said Mr Carter. "OK. Here we go!"

They crowded round the envelope, a bit like TV and film stars do when they're announcing an award. Mr Carter ripped the top off it. He took out a piece of paper and held it up.

"I can't look!" said Dionna, shutting her eyes. "Is it Good?"

"It isn't," said Ryan.

"Oh no!" said Dionna sadly. "Inadequate. Again. Oh no, oh no . . ."

"Not that either," said Ryan.

"OMG – they haven't created a Rubbish rating, have they?"

"Dionna," said Mr Carter gently. "Open your eyes."

Dionna apparently still wasn't convinced this was a good idea, so just opened one. But when she saw what was written on the paper, she thought she must have read it wrongly, that it was some kind of one-eyed misunderstanding. It was the same, though, when she opened the other one. So it must be true.

"OUTSTANDING?" she said.

"YES!" said Ryan.

"THAT'S AMAZING!" said Dionna.

"WOW!" said Ryan. "That really *is* amazing!"

"It is," said Mr Carter. "I did make sure to provide OFFHEAD with a bit of extra information, of course. For example, that since your little stint in the job, the pupils at this school have become *better*, would you believe, at handing in homework and coming up with great ideas for class activities. They're generally more disciplined too! It's as if – as if you gave them a little holiday . . . from . . . well, from a rather stuffy idea of what school should be. And they enjoyed that and have come back as model schoolchildren!"

Ryan nodded, surprised, but pleased.

"But you know what? I think mainly," Mr Carter said, folding up the bit of paper, "it was about what you two were like at the debate. Those speeches you made were inspiring – they saved the school!"

Dionna and Ryan looked at each other.

"I suppose we did!" said Ryan.

"Hey!" said Dionna, raising her palm.

"High-five? Bit normo."

"Do it."

He slapped her palm, smiling.

"On which note," said Mr Carter, "this school needs a head pupil. We haven't had one before.

Most schools do and I was wondering if maybe . . .
you . . . ?"

"Well," said Ryan. "It's been an amazing journey
for me, the naughtiest boy in the school. But, hey . . .
yes, Mr Carter — I'd be happy to. I'd be happy to be
head boy."

Mr Carter nodded. And then said, "Not you, you
big wally. Dionna! Of course. I'm offering her head
girl!"

"You are?" said Dionna.

"You are?" said Ryan.

Mr Carter nodded. Dionna smiled.

"Hey! Yes! Thank you. Why not?"

"Why not indeed, Dionna!"

"Wow," said Ryan a little sheepishly. "Head kid!
Cool."

She looked out of the window. Parents had
started arriving to pick up their children. "Can I go
and tell my mum? I think she'll be really proud."

"Of course!"

And she ran back out to the playground. Mr Carter and Ryan looked at each other for a moment. Then Mr Carter burst out laughing, a big pointed "HA! HA! HA! HA! HA!"

"*You*, my friend, just got pranked! You are SO lame! You are one dank meme!"

Now it was Ryan's turn to smile. "Good one. Not as good as your onstage cake-mix prank, obviously."

"Yes, that *was* amazing!"

"Top drawer. Getting the containers up there must have been tough."

"It was. But I was committed."

"You were. But I gotta say, you had me with that head-boy thing." He pointed an index finger at Mr Carter and said, "Keep pranking, bro. One day you might be at my level!"

And then he turned to go out into the playground.

"Ryan!" said Mr Carter.

Ryan turned back.

"Just *one more* one-more thing." Mr Carter reached out a hand. For a second, Ryan was a bit worried – was he going to slap him? Was he still annoyed? But then he grabbed hold of Ryan's tie, dangling two buttons down his neck as ever, not properly tied.

"Here," he said, and pulled it tight up to Ryan's collar. Mr Carter stood back and admired his handiwork. "At last," he said.

Ryan felt his tie, made a *whatevs* face and looked up. "OK, sure," he said. "But I think this –" he reached out and pulled Mr Carter's tie *down* a notch so it hung loosely on him for once – "might now suit *you* a bit better!"

Mr Carter smiled. He glanced into the mirror above the fireplace – the same one Mr Barrington had looked at to try to work out the words on his forehead a little while ago – and said, "You know what, Ryan? I think you might be right!"

Ryan nodded. Then he turned and ran out towards the playground.

Mr Carter watched him go, dodging all the footballers and fights and hopscotches and hand-held video-gaming and climbing of climbing frames going on, towards his mum. Tina Ward, in fact, saw Mr Carter looking out from his window, and waved and smiled at him in a friendly way. He waved back, remembering something from when he was Ryan, already becoming a little dim in his memory, what she'd said about wanting him to tell her something real about himself: about Mr Carter, that is. About what he was like as a person.

Maybe, he thought, *I'll try and do that tomorrow*.

But for now he had things to do. He had to sort out tomorrow's assembly, to check on the supply-teacher availabilities, to organise a meeting of the board of governors and, indeed, to write an announcement celebrating the school's new OFFHEAD rating.

Just before he sat down at his computer to type, though, he noticed something on his desk. And he remembered what Ryan had just said before leaving his office.

Keep pranking, bro.

He picked up the object from the desk.

He knew *exactly* what to do.

Coda

"**B**ELINDA! THANK YOU FOR COMING INTO MY OFFICE! I WANTED TO SHOW YOU THIS!"

"What is it, Mrs Valentine-Fine OBE?"

"IT JUST ARRIVED TODAY FROM THAT TERRIBLE MR CARTER MAN AT THAT AWFUL BRACKET WOOD PLACE. I SUPPOSE IT MIGHT BE SOME KIND OF PEACE OFFERING. SOME WAY OF SAYING SORRY."

"Yes, I suppose it might. It's a box, is it?"

"YES, WITH SOME KIND OF ARROW DESIGN ON IT! RATHER BEAUTIFUL, CERTAINLY, COMING FROM THAT PLACE."

"It's a musical box, I think. Can't find the key. Hmm. Let me give it a bit of a bang down on the desk."

BANG! WHIRR.

"ALL RIGHT. HMM. I SUPPOSE THAT IS QUITE A NICE TU—"

Thanks to:

Nick Lake – the man at the editorial coal face.

Ann-Janine Murtagh – the woman who got me into writing books for children, and who continues to fire me up to write more.

Steven Lenton – my new amazing illustrator.

Georgia Garrett – my always amazing agent.

Morwenna Banks – for everything, as ever, but specifically for some great story suggestions on this one.

Tanya Hougham – audio book above and beyond-er.

David McDougall and Elorine Grant – design maestros.

Sam Stewart – corrector of errors.

And everyone else at HarperCollins who helps to make these books and get them out into the world.